About the a

Elen Caldecott graduated with an MA in Writing for Young People from Bath Spa University. Before becoming a writer, she was an archaeologist, a nurse, a theatre usher and a museum security guard. It was while working at the museum that Elen realised there is a way to steal anything if you think about it hard enough. Elen either had to become a master thief, or create some characters to do it for her – and so her debut novel, *How Kirsty Jenkins Stole the Elephant*, was born. It was shortlisted for the Waterstones Children's Prize and was followed by *How Ali Ferguson Saved Houdini* and *Operation Eiffel Tower*. Elen lives in Bristol with her husband, Simon, and their dog.

www.elencaldecott.com

Check out the **Elen Caldecott Children's Author** page on Facebook

Also by Elen Caldecott

How Kirsty Jenkins Stole the Elephant

How Ali Ferguson Saved Houdini

Operation Eiffel Tower

The Mystery of Wickworth Manor

The Great Ice-Cream Heist

DIAMONDS and DAGGERS

The Marsh Road Mysteries

Diamonds and Daggers

ELEN CALDECOTT

BLOOMSBURY
LONDON NEW DELHI NEW YORK SYDNEY

Bloomsbury Publishing, London, New Delhi, New York and Sydney

First published in Great Britain in February 2015 by Bloomsbury Publishing Plc
50 Bedford Square, London WC1B 3DP

www.bloomsbury.com
www.elencaldecott.com

Bloomsbury is a registered trademark of Bloomsbury Publishing Plc

A CIP catalogue record for this book is available from the British Library

ISBN 978 1 4088 4752 7

Typeset by Hewer Text UK Ltd, Edinburgh
Printed and bound in Great Britain by CPI Group (UK) Ltd, Croydon CR0 4YY

1 3 5 7 9 10 8 6 4 2

To Monika and Karolina, dziękuję

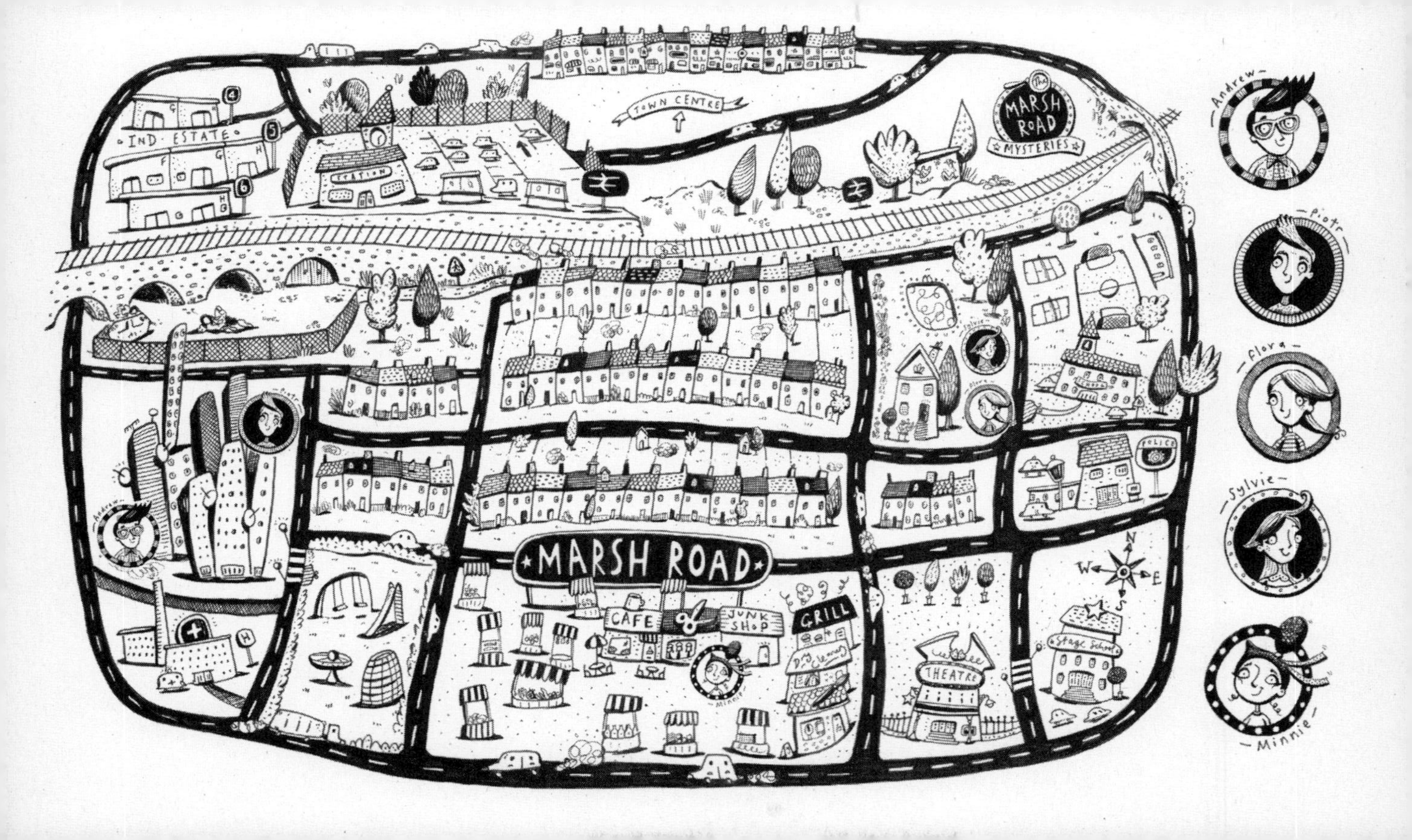
The MARSH ROAD MYSTERIES
TOWN CENTRE
IND ESTATE
STATION
POLICE
MARSH ROAD
CAFE
JUNK SHOP
GRILL
Dry Cleaners
THEATRE
Stage School
N
S
E
W
Andrew
Piotr
Flora
Sylvie
Minnie

Chapter One

Piotr Domek was pretending not to look. He sat with his back to the salon window, pretending he hadn't a care in the world, pretending this was any other regular, normal, ordinary kind of day. He wasn't watching the street outside. No way. He couldn't let Minnie think that. The only reason he had the mirror angled in his hand was because he was checking his fringe. He wasn't using the mirror to keep a careful, fixed, watchful eye on the street. Definitely not.

'You're watching, aren't you?' Minnie asked.

Minnie knew him very well.

Piotr and Minnie and Andrew had been friends since the first day of playgroup, when Andrew had painted them all blue before the nursery nurse noticed and they all had to be changed into lost-property clothes. Hanging out with Andrew had meant a lot of lost-property clothes over the years.

'I'm not watching,' Piotr lied.

'You are.'

'Am not.'

'Are too.'

They might have carried on like that all day, or at least until teatime, if Minnie's mum hadn't come out of the back room of the salon to tell them to be quiet. 'I'm on the phone with a supplier and I can't hear myself think,' she said.

Piotr and Minnie clamped their mouths shut. Minnie sat back down by the nail bar. There were no customers booked in, so she could reorganise her mum's nail varnishes however she liked. 'I'm going to arrange them by which looks the most like poison,' she whispered. She picked up a jet-black bottle first.

Piotr leaned back in the window seat, pushing a copy of *Afro Hair* magazine out of the way. He angled the mirror again. Minnie made a snorty noise. Piotr ignored her.

Outside, reflected in the glass, he could see Marsh Road market in full swing. The pedestrianised zone was busy with shoppers.

Then he saw a small figure in the distance, running. The small figure was waving something above its head.

Piotr tried not to look around. Minnie would tease him forever if he did. The figure in the mirror turned into a short, white boy, wearing glasses, with dark hair flopping all over the place as he ran.

Andrew.

Piotr tried to sit still. He tried to look bored. He tried to –

Piotr dropped the mirror on the seat, flipped around and stared out of the window. 'He's coming!'

Minnie paused with a bottle of green, glittery gunk in her hand. 'I knew it! You were looking! Ha! You do know he's going to be a nightmare now, don't you?'

Piotr watched Andrew pelting towards them. The object above his head was a newspaper and he waved it as though he were batting off a swarm of wasps.

Andrew burst into the salon.

His normally moon-pale face was pink from the effort of running. And breathing. And trying to speak. He couldn't manage all three. He waved the newspaper instead.

'She's here,' he finally managed to wheeze.

'Who?' Minnie teased.

'Who? *Who?* Look! *She's* here!' He unfolded the paper so that they could see the front page. 'Betty Massino, world-famous actress, star of blockbuster hits like

Breakout on Mars and *Toy Club*, Oscar nominated, walker of red carpets and papped by paparazzi everywhere. Betty Massino. *The* Betty Massino! She's only gone and arrived in our town!' Andrew clutched the newspaper to his chest as if he were accepting an Oscar.

'Betty Massino … Betty Massino,' Minnie muttered. 'Yes, I think I might have heard that name before.'

'Argh!' Andrew gave a cry of pure frustration.

Minnie got up from the nail bar and snatched the newspaper from Andrew's hands like a seagull nabbing chips from a pigeon.

'Oi!'

She danced away from him, across the black and white tiles, towards the basins. Andrew leaped after her. She held the paper up, towards the display of wigs and hair extensions and wraps. Andrew, yelling now, jumped as high as he could to get it back. But Minnie was a good foot taller. He had no chance.

Minnie's mum called from the treatment room at the back of the shop. 'What's going on there? Do I need to come out?'

Minnie stopped straight, as if Mum had flicked a switch. She handed the newspaper back to Andrew. Minnie knew Mum was on the phone to Big Phil; even his name made Mum frown every time she said it. Bothering Mum now was deadly.

Andrew carried a cloud of sulk with him as he smoothed down the paper.

'Show me,' Piotr said.

Piotr hadn't got up from the window seat. Usually, it was best to leave Minnie and Andrew to it when they fought. Although they looked so different, they were identical when it came to bickering.

Piotr flattened the paper on his lap. His two friends sat on either side of him and peered in.

The front page showed a photo of Betty Massino arriving outside the theatre at the end of the street. Piotr felt a shiver of excitement. Nothing like Andrew's full-blown, verging-on-a-heart-attack frenzy, but a thrill just the same.

In the photo, Betty was stepping out of a black car, waving and smiling at the camera. Her dark hair was swept up and her eyes sparkled with glee. A young man in a dark grey jumper held her luggage. They were both in front of the Theatre Grande, less than three minutes' walk from Minnie's mum's salon.

A Hollywood actress here! Piotr could hardly believe it. It felt like a twinkling star had fallen from the night sky and landed in Marsh Road. Nothing as brilliant as this had ever happened in their sleepy little town before.

'Read it,' Andrew instructed.

Piotr did as he was told. '"Betty Massino, star of stage and screen, arrived this morning at the Theatre Grande to join the cast of *The Road to Moscow*. Betty is temporarily returning to the town where her grandparents lived before emigrating to America. Seen here with her assistant, Ms Massino will take the lead role of tragic widow, Natasha Arcadina. Ms Massino told reporters that she feels she's come home and can't wait to begin rehearsals."'

Andrew's grin was huge. This was the best thing ever.

'Betty's here ... so?' Minnie asked.

'So? *So?*' Andrew was indignant. 'Is that all you can say? This is only about the most exciting, most astounding thing that's ever happened to us in our whole lifetimes.'

'But it hasn't happened to us, has it? She's just in town.'

'This will change the summer.'

'It changes nothing.'

'A celebrity in town!'

'In town, not in our lives!'

Piotr let them slug it out. He picked up the now-forgotten paper and looked at the photo. Betty had a nice smile, friendly. Travelling hadn't given her a crinkly face from falling asleep on a pile of coats, the way it did normal people.

'Piotr's dad can!'

Piotr looked up as Andrew said his name. He hadn't been listening. 'My dad can what?' he asked.

Andrew gave another dramatic sigh. 'I *said* that your dad can introduce us. He works at the theatre.'

Piotr sighed. Not this again. Andrew had been talking about Dad's job for weeks and weeks, ever since he learned Betty was coming. This had 'lost-property-clothing disaster' written all over it.

'Dad can't introduce us. He works as security,' Piotr said. 'He's always on the stage door. He never goes anywhere near the actual stage – you know that.'

It wasn't as if they hadn't had this conversation about two hundred billion times already this holiday.

Andrew clasped his hands together, in a silent prayer. 'But he could this once, couldn't he? For us? You'll ask him, won't you?' Andrew fell to his knees, begging Piotr to do this one, tiny, small, totally impossible thing.

Minnie tutted. 'You'll get covered in hair clippings if you roll around down there. I haven't swept up yet.'

'Please say you'll ask him. Please? Pretty please with bows on?'

Piotr glanced at the photo. Could he ask Dad to introduce them to Betty? 'Even if I did ask, he'd say no,' Piotr said.

'Does that mean you'll ask?' Andrew said. 'Yes!' He punched the air.

Piotr hung his head. He'd walked right into that. He was an idiot. Now, Andrew wasn't going to let it drop, ever. 'Dad won't do it, though, I'm telling you.'

'Will you ask him now?' Andrew bounded up.

'You want to go to the theatre now?' Piotr frowned. It was usually better to ask Dad for things in more roundabout ways. Subtle. Planned. Not just tearing in like a hyperactive whirlwind. Dad wasn't mean, not at all. He just preferred to stick to the rules, to do things by the book.

'Yes,' Andrew said. 'We should go right now. This could be it – my big Hollywood break. If I can impress Betty then she might let me have a role in her next film. I could be the next James Bond.'

'You could be the next James Pond,' Minnie muttered.

Andrew looked so hopeful that Piotr found he felt a tiny bit hopeful too. Maybe Dad *would* let them into the theatre. Maybe he *would* take them to Betty Massino's dressing room. Maybe Andrew *would* get to play the most famous spy ever, running around stopping baddies and saving the world. Yes, and maybe that was a flying pig hovering over Marsh Road.

Piotr sighed. 'Don't get your hopes up.'

Andrew whooped.

'I said, don't get your hopes up!'

Minnie went to the back to tell Mum they were leaving.

Then the three headed out to try and meet one of the most famous people in the world.

Chapter Two

Minnie's mum's salon was sandwiched right in the middle of a row of shops, set back from Marsh Road market. On one side of the salon was a cafe that served hot, buttered toast to customers sitting in squeaky-plastic booths. On the other side was a junk shop, selling old furniture and crockery and battered pots and pans. Beyond that a newsagent's and health-food shop. The market stalls formed a bright welcome mat to the shops. There were fruit stalls that smelled of sugar and sunshine; flower stalls with more colours than a kaleidoscope; clothes stalls, shoe stalls; second-hand book and knick-knack stalls, with traders yelling, 'Two for a pound!' so loudly that it sounded more like, 'Doofrabound, doofrabound!'

Piotr, Minnie and Andrew left the salon and rushed through the market. All around them people were going about their shopping business, trundling tartan trolleys or lugging blue plastic bags that dug into their wrists.

But there was no time for browsing.

Andrew raced ahead, like a missile set on a target.

Poor Betty Massino, Piotr thought. She had no idea what was heading her way. Neither did Dad.

The theatre was at the end of the market, where the road widened into a small square, edged by flaking plane trees. The theatre was a huge, cream building. Thick columns like a giant's wrists held up the carved roof.

Andrew headed towards the wide, white steps.

'No,' Piotr said. 'This way.'

Dad worked at the back of the theatre.

Piotr led them around the side of the building. Here, the creamy facade gave way to mottled red brick and the road narrowed to little more than an alley.

The stage door was where the cast and crew slipped into the building, away from the goggling eyes of the audience.

Piotr went first. He could sense Andrew bouncing on the soles of his feet, eager to meet a Hollywood legend. He knew that Minnie was hanging back a little, not so certain that this was a good idea.

She was probably right.

The door was heavy. It opened on to a dark lobby. A high desk, painted black, but with the paint chipped and peeling, filled most of the space.

A man with dark brown hair, dark eyes and a frown sat behind the desk. His black jumper blended so well with the desk that in the gloom it looked like his severed head floated in mid-air. Behind him, on the wall, hung a row of clipboards and keys.

'Dad?' Piotr whispered.

'Piotrek?' Dad sounded alarmed. '*Coś nie tak?* Is it your mother? Or Kasia?' Normally Dad would have spoken English so that Andrew and Minnie would understand. He was always very polite like that. But worry made him speak Polish.

Piotr felt his cheeks redden. Of course Dad would think there was something wrong with Mum or his sister. Why else would Piotr be here? 'No, no, they're fine …' he replied in English.

'Then, why … ?' Dad gestured with his hands, turning the wave into a question.

Andrew bounced forward. 'Hi, Mr Domek, how are you doing? Have you seen her? Is she here?'

Dad tutted. 'Good afternoon, Andrew. So, it isn't just journalists and photographers I have to deal with, no? It's you too?' He looked seriously at his son. 'You shouldn't be here. It's a very busy day – I need to work.'

Piotr glanced at the scuffed ground. It was no use. Dad was usually great, but rules were rules. Actually, rules were more like solid brick walls that couldn't be knocked down, or bent, or even stepped around. *Of course* Dad wasn't going to let them into Betty Massino's dressing room. It was just another one of Andrew's daft schemes.

He was about to turn and herd the others out on to the street – he'd never hear the end of this from Dad *or* Andrew – when the door leading from the theatre into the lobby opened.

The three froze. Stared at the opening door.

Betty Massino? Could it be?

No. It wasn't.

It was a girl, about their own age. She had milk-white skin, with a cinnamon splattering of freckles, ginger-biscuit hair and china-blue eyes. She made Piotr think of afternoon tea at a smart hotel.

Piotr smiled at her shyly.

The girl ignored him completely.

She stepped up to his dad.

'I've lost my ID badge,' she snapped. No hello, no good morning, no nothing.

Piotr's mouth fell open. He waited for Dad to give her the sharp telling-off that Piotr would get if he spoke to an adult that way.

Dad didn't speak.

'I need a new one,' the girl said impatiently.

Dad flushed and looked down at the desk. Even his neck was turning red.

Piotr felt squirmy all of a sudden. Embarrassed. For Dad? It was a horrible feeling, as though all the air had been pushed out of his chest. 'Let's go,' he whispered.

Minnie was going nowhere. She put both her hands on her hips. She set her feet slightly apart. 'What's the magic word?' she said.

The girl didn't react at all – it was as if Minnie hadn't spoken.

'Hey!' Minnie said.

Mr Domek gave her a sharp look. Minnie felt her face redden. 'Well, she thinks she's the Queen of Sheba,' Minnie protested. Not that Minnie knew where Sheba was, but it was something Mum said all the time.

'We've talked about this, Sylvie,' Mr Domek said finally to the girl. 'You need to take better care of your things.'

Sylvie shrugged.

Just then, Andrew pointed to a cord that hung from the back pocket of Sylvie's skirt. 'What's that?' he asked.

Sylvie didn't move.

'Hey, you,' Andrew tried again. 'There's something square in your back pocket. What is it?'

Sylvie felt inside her pocket. She pulled out a laminated card attached to the black cord. 'Oh,' she said, then shrugged. 'I suppose you don't have to make me a new one.'

She hung her badge around her neck.

'Take better care of it,' Dad said softly.

She walked back through the door into the theatre without another word.

There was silence in the lobby.

Piotr felt his eyes prickle hotly. He had never seen Dad treated like that before, never. Not by anyone.

'You should go,' Dad said to them. 'You shouldn't be here.'

Andrew broke the tension. 'You wouldn't throw us out in the freezing cold, would you, Mr Domek? Not without saying a tiny hello to Betty Massino?'

It was blazing summer sunshine outside.

Dad laughed weakly, despite himself. 'Andrew, I'm sorry to tell you that I would. Now, come on, out.'

He was ready to usher them out into the street when the theatre door opened again.

Was it that hateful girl? Piotr felt his skin tingle, ready, this time, to tell her exactly what he thought of her.

No.

It wasn't Sylvie.

The door was pushed wide open.

A woman stepped into the lobby. She had dark hair and creamy skin and was wearing workout leggings.

Betty Massino.

Andrew yelped like someone had run over his foot. Then he smiled as wide as he could. It gave him the look of a deranged shark.

Minnie gasped.

And Piotr just stared.

Betty noticed them standing like lemons and grinned impishly. She looked younger than Piotr had expected. Her dark hair was pulled back into a ponytail and it didn't look like she had make-up on. She looked ready for work.

'Mr Domek?' she said to Dad. 'Sir, I wonder whether you could help me, please? I'll need a cab booked for the moment rehearsals are over.'

'Certainly, I can do that. Where would you like to go?'

'To my hotel, via the bank. The manager has agreed to

stay open a little longer than usual so I can deposit my necklace for safekeeping, but I don't want to keep him any later than I have to. So, could you ask the driver to be prompt?'

Her American accent sounded as exotic as passion fruit, as exciting as a Christmas feast. Piotr could barely breathe.

'I can do that,' Dad said.

'Thank you,' Betty said. 'And who are our visitors?'

'My son. His friends.'

'Welcome to the theatre!' Betty said with a wink. Then she disappeared back behind the door.

'Wow!' Andrew sighed. 'Wow! Wow! Wow! Betty Massino just winked at me. This has absolutely been the best day of my life. This was better than the time we went bungee jumping for my birthday and I forgot about the can in my pocket and it sprayed everyone in a fizz fountain.'

Another lost-property-clothes day.

Meeting Betty Massino almost made Piotr forget about the girl who had been so rude to Dad. Almost.

Chapter Three

'We met Betty Massino,' Andrew said as they walked back towards the market. 'Do you think she liked me? Do you think she was impressed?'

Minnie snorted. 'Andrew, you were in the same room as her for precisely ten seconds. You've spent longer buying a packet of crisps. So, no, I don't think she was impressed.'

'We were there long enough for her to wink at us!'

Piotr gave a small grin. Meeting Betty had been amazing, but he couldn't help remembering that girl, Sylvie. The way she'd spoken to Dad and he'd just stood there. Dad sometimes said people treated him like an idiot, just because he spoke with an accent. But Piotr had never seen it for himself. The memory hurt, like sunburn ruining a day at the beach.

Andrew leaped up on bollards and twirled around

lamp posts as he walked. 'I can't stay out,' he said. 'I want to go and tell Mum what happened. She had an early physio appointment so I'm cooking tea. Jacket potatoes and beans.'

Piotr knew Andrew was helping his mum a lot these days; she wasn't well. He also knew that Andrew would love telling his mum – the story would get bigger and bigger and bigger. Eventually, he'd say that they hadn't just met Betty, but she'd taken them inside and shown them her dressing room and decided they were all friends and promised them first-class tickets to New York. Andrew's stories were like that.

Minnie had to get home too. So Piotr made his way back to the flat alone.

He liked this time of day, late afternoon, before the streets swelled with people coming home from work. The sun spreading a gentle heat like butter on toast. Even the smells were good – hot tarmac, market strawberries, the spices and tangs of early cooking. He tried to forget Sylvie.

At the flats the lift was working. Good. He hated lift-broken days, when he had to climb five flights of stairs. It had been worse when his little sister Kasia was a baby and they'd had to carry her pushchair up too. She was old enough to walk now, but still liked to be carried on lift-broken days.

Mum was home, playing with Kasia. '*Hej, Pietrucha*,' Mum said. Piotr grinned. If Mum ever called him Piotr, he was in trouble. If she called him Piotrek, it was middling. But if she called him Pietrucha – Parsley – that meant she'd had a good day.

'*Hej, Mama. Hej, Kasia.*'

His sister waved a plastic truck at him. Piotr played with her for a while. Mostly that just meant letting her pull toys out of a crate while he put them back in again. He didn't mind. Kasia laughed at everything, so she was easy to like.

'We'll be eating soon. Would you set the table?' Mum said.

The table was a fold-up one that lived down the side of the sofa. Piotr lifted it free and set it up. Kasia had a high chair. He and Mum had fold-out chairs. Kasia smeared as much potato on her face as she got in her mouth, but she chuckled while Mum pulled food out of her eyebrows, so Piotr had to smile.

Dad wouldn't come home until after bedtime.

After tea, Mum bathed Kasia and read her a story. Piotr was allowed to stay up for an hour or two to watch TV.

Later, Piotr said goodnight and Mum switched off his bedroom light. He lay in the dark for a while, listening to the night-time sounds. The window was open a tiny bit, to let in fresh air. He could hear traffic and the faint sounds of people in the street below. He turned on to his side, switched on his torch and read for a while.

Dad wasn't home by the time Piotr finished his comic.

That was weird.

He checked the clock beside his bed. Dad was late.

He always came in to say goodnight and to tell Piotr to switch off his torch.

Piotr fished another comic out from under his bed. It was one he'd read before. But he didn't want to go to sleep before Dad got home.

It was nearly an hour later that Piotr heard Dad's key in the lock. He wondered whether to turn off his torch before Dad told him to.

But Dad didn't come into his room.

Instead, Piotr heard him walk slowly down the narrow corridor, past the two bedrooms, to the living room at the end. His footsteps were heavy.

Then Piotr heard the sound of urgent, hushed words. Rapid Polish rattled from the living room.

This wasn't like Dad at all.

What was going on?

Why was he home so late?

Piotr drew back his duvet and stood up slowly, careful not to make a sound. He opened his bedroom door a crack and concentrated as hard as he could on the voices in the living room. He made out clipped phrases, 'can't believe it … outrageous … how could they think it … last straw.' Dad's voice was low, so as not to wake Kasia, but it was sharp as glass.

Piotr risked opening the door a little further.

What *was* going on?

Dad must have sensed the motion, or heard a sound, because he called out, 'Piotr? Is that you?'

Piotr sighed. Busted.

He walked slowly into the living room, his head down.

'I'm sorry,' Dad said, 'I didn't mean to wake you.'

Piotr felt a jolt of surprise; he'd been expecting some sharp words about not listening to adult conversations.

'Come here.' Dad opened his arms and waved Piotr closer. Piotr sat on the sofa and let himself lean against the solid bulk of his father's shoulders. It was like leaning against a kindly bear. Dad gave him a small squeeze. Piotr was too old for hugs really, but that didn't stop it feeling nice.

He glanced over at Mum. She was frowning. A heavy crease between her eyebrows made her look sad.

Dad stroked Piotr's head. 'Piotrek, you're a good boy. But this isn't a good place for you,' Dad whispered.

'What do you mean?' A sliver of worry sprang up inside. This didn't feel at all like being told off for being out of bed.

Mum flashed a look at Dad. 'Pawel.' She made Dad's name a warning.

'No, Magda – the boy needs to know.' Dad relaxed the hug and looked Piotr directly in the eye. 'Son, something happened at work today. Something serious. Betty Massino was going to call at the bank this evening after rehearsal. She was going to give them a diamond necklace for safekeeping. She didn't get to the bank. And the necklace has disappeared from the theatre.'

Poor Betty! Piotr remembered the friendly wink she'd given them. What a horrible thing to happen. 'How? Where did it go?' Piotr asked.

Dad didn't answer straightaway. Piotr could see that the muscles in his jaw were clenched tight. Dad drew a hand across his chin. 'The police came,' Dad said. 'They scoured the theatre from top to bottom. They searched everyone, every bag and pocket. They even brought a sniffer dog. I –' Dad's voice broke. But he paused, took a breath and continued. 'They think it was stolen. I was in charge of security. It happened on my watch.'

'But it isn't your fault,' Piotr said. Of course it wasn't Dad's fault!

Dad shook his head. 'Someone told the police they saw me near Ms Massino's dressing room. Security have keys for the whole building.' Dad dropped his head into his hands. 'I'm a suspect. I've been suspended from work.'

The room was silent.

Piotr couldn't process his thoughts quickly enough. Suspended? Like from school? But Dad wasn't at school.

Mum stood up, came over to the sofa and wrapped her arms around Dad. She held him for a moment, then she said, 'Coffee. You need something warm and sweet.'

She moved towards the kitchen, but Dad called to her. 'It's the last straw, Magda. It's the end.'

Mum paused in the middle of the room.

Piotr wrapped his arms around his own shoulders. It was cold out of bed.

'What do you mean?' Mum asked. 'What are you saying, Pawel?'

Dad looked tired as he raised his head, the skin around his eyes grey and puffy. 'We've talked about it enough. I don't want to stay in a country that doesn't want me, that doesn't respect me. I did not steal that necklace. You know that. But they take someone else's word over mine. I was not near that dressing room. Well, I have no intention of staying in a place where I am not trusted. I have always said this country is not our home. So, I have decided we are leaving.'

Dad rested a hand on Piotr's shoulder. 'We're going back to Poland.'

Chapter Four

Piotr shook off Dad's hand. 'Poland? I'm not going to Poland.'

Mum stepped closer. 'Pawel, we need to talk about this. Piotr, go back to bed.'

Piotr looked at his parents. 'You can't decide this without me!'

A look of sadness flashed across Dad's face. 'This isn't a good place.'

'But it's home!'

'Piotr, bed. Now.' Mum's voice was firm. 'Your father and I must discuss this.'

There was no arguing. At least not tonight. Piotr held his own elbows, and dodged the kiss that Mum tried to drop on his forehead. He wished he could slam the door, but that would just make Dad more cross.

Poland.

Poland?

Piotr lay in the dark, staring up at the pale ceiling. The pillow felt as uncomfortable as a brick beneath his head. There was no way he could sleep. There was no way he could go and live in Poland. He'd been there a few times, on holiday, to see relatives; it had been fun. But it wasn't home. It had never been home, not to him.

He could hear his parents talking late into the night. Soft voices, whispering through the thin wall between their rooms. Mum's voice soothing, Dad's brittle and angry.

Sleep came, finally, like falling down a well.

The sun was well and truly up, giving the curtains a bright halo, when a knock at the front door woke him.

He blinked for a moment, wondering who might be visiting so early. Then he remembered, Dad, the necklace, Poland. He was awake in an instant. He pulled on his jeans and tugged a hoodie over his pyjama top. Then he went into the hall.

Mum was already at the door.

Two police officers, one man, one woman, stood on the doorstep. Piotr thought he recognised the man from around the estate. Or maybe he'd talked to them about crossing the road safely in Year Two?

Kasia ran into the hallway on her chubby legs. She giggled at Piotr as he grabbed for her.

'Piotrek,' Mum said, 'take your sister out for a while.'

'What? Why?'

'Please. Just do it.'

He wanted to stay. Wanted to know why the police were here. Had they found the necklace? Or were they here to arrest Dad?

The man must have seen the fear in his eyes. 'We're just here to take a statement, that's all,' he said.

'Please, Piotrek.' Mum sounded tired, worried.

Piotr nodded. 'Come on, Kasia. Where are your shoes?'

There was a small play park with swings and a little slide just outside the flats. Kasia's absolute favourite was a wobbly chicken on a spring. Piotr propped her up inside the chicken and listened to her giggle as she wobbled. She had no idea of the catastrophe they were facing.

'Piotr!'

Piotr looked up from the chicken.

'Piotr!' Andrew and Minnie swung open the yellow gate that separated the play park from the street. 'Piotr! Did you hear the news? A robbery at the theatre!' Andrew grabbed the wobbly frog that crouched next to

Kasia's wobbly chicken and tried to sit on it. He fell straight off.

'Stop it,' Minnie said. 'It's meant for toddlers.'

'Did you hear?' Andrew asked again, righting his glasses and ignoring Minnie. 'It wasn't just in the local paper. It was on the news! On the telly! Betty's diamond necklace vanished last night. Twelve diamonds each the size of a bottle top. They showed a clip of her wearing them at the Oscars. Do you know how much diamonds that size are worth?' Having a celebrity in town was just getting more and more exciting as far as Andrew was concerned.

'Piotr, are you OK?' Minnie asked. His head was down. He pushed Kasia's chicken as though he were completing a prison sentence.

Piotr nodded warily.

'What's the matter?'

Piotr shrugged.

'Babysitting?' Andrew nodded towards Kasia.

'She's no trouble.' It was true. Kasia chirruped away happily as the chicken swayed.

'What then?'

If he said it out loud, then it would make it real. Like casting an evil spell and making a demon appear.

'The police are asking questions all around the market,' Minnie said. 'The necklace has just disappeared into thin air. Did your dad tell you about it?'

Piotr had no idea how to share what Dad had said. It was too big, too horrible.

Piotr lifted his sister from the wobbly chicken and held her close. She struggled for a second, but then threw her chubby arms around his neck. 'We're going,' he said.

'Now?' Andrew asked. 'We've only just got here!'

'No,' Piotr replied. 'I mean we're going. Really going. My dad wants to take us to Poland. For good.'

There was a stunned silence. Minnie and Andrew looked across at each other, eyes wide in exactly the same expression of shock.

'But why?' Minnie asked.

'He's upset.' Piotr found it hard to carry on speaking, but Minnie and Andrew were his best friends, he had to tell them, so he forced the words out. 'The police think Dad did it. He was reported near the scene. He's their main suspect.'

The silence broke like a wave hitting rocks. Minnie and Andrew chorused their horror together.

'He wouldn't do that!'

'That's not right. It can't be.'

'Your dad would never have.'

Kasia squeezed her arms tighter around Piotr's neck and he hoisted her into a more comfortable position. He could smell the baby bath bubbles his parents washed her in.

He didn't know what to say to his friends. Their anger made him feel a tiny bit better – they didn't believe it either – but it didn't change the fact that Dad was talking about leaving.

'You can't go,' Minnie said finally.

'I don't want to!' Piotr snapped. 'It isn't fair.'

'Maybe he'll calm down,' Andrew said hopefully. 'When my mum thinks I've done something stupid, she can be cross for hours, but she cheers up eventually.'

'This isn't the same,' Piotr said.

'Hey!' The shout came from the entrance to the flats. Piotr turned and saw one of the police officers waving to him. It was the man. The woman headed towards their squad car.

The police officer waved again.

'What does he want?' Minnie said.

'He really wants to talk to you.' Andrew leaned against the vacant chicken.

Piotr carried Kasia to the edge of the play park and stood behind the railings. The police officer was just a few metres away. He was a tall man, with light brown hair and a wide mouth that looked close to smiling.

'Hello,' the man said.

'Hello,' Piotr replied warily.

'I'm Special Constable Wright. I usually do the beat in this part of town. You can call me Jimmy.'

Right now, Piotr didn't want to call him anything.

Jimmy's face broke into a sad smile. 'It's a difficult time, I understand.'

'My dad didn't do it!' Piotr burst out suddenly. He couldn't stand the pity on the special constable's face.

'Why do you think that?'

Kasia cried out angrily. He was holding her too tight. He forced himself to calm down. 'Because,' Piotr said quietly, 'my dad is a good man. The best. He would never steal anything.'

Jimmy looked thoughtful. 'He doesn't seem a likely candidate. But the trouble is, the evidence points to him.'

'What evidence?'

'I can't say,' Jimmy shrugged. 'Not while the enquiry is going on. Listen, if you or your mum need anything … your dad is pretty upset … if I can help at all, get in touch. And if anything occurs to you …' He reached into his pocket and pulled out a small white card. He handed it to Piotr.

Piotr took it.

'You're the police, right?' Andrew's voice was closer than Piotr had expected. He looked over his shoulder. Andrew and Minnie had come to stand right by him.

Jimmy grinned at Andrew. 'I'm a special constable.'

'Same thing,' Andrew said. 'Piotr's dad didn't do it, but he wants to go back to Poland because you think he did. Can you stop him?'

'What do you mean?' Jimmy asked.

'Can't you say –' Andrew put on his best American accent – '"Don't go leaving town."'

'You've been watching too many films,' Jimmy said. 'He can leave if he wants to. Unless he's arrested.' Jimmy blushed. 'Sorry. But your dad is one line of enquiry ... Take care now. Look after your sister.'

Jimmy turned and walked back to the squad car.

Piotr looked at Jimmy's name on the card. He nearly crumpled it up and threw it at the bin, but something made him stop. He put it into his back pocket.

'They still think Dad did it,' Piotr said softly.

'But he didn't,' Andrew said.

Piotr looked at his two best friends. He couldn't leave them. 'Dad's talked about going back to Poland, but he meant when he was old. To retire. This is different. This time he means it. If the police don't find the real thief, we're leaving.'

'They'll find the real thief,' Andrew said. 'And Betty Massino will get her necklace back, you'll see.'

'But what if they don't?'

'Well,' Minnie said, 'if they don't find the thief, we'll just have to do it for them.'

Chapter Five

'Do it for them?' Andrew asked.

'Yes.' Minnie's eyes sparkled as the thought became clearer. Piotr couldn't be whisked off to Poland that easily. 'If the police are convinced that Mr Domek stole the necklace, then they won't bother looking for the real criminal. The thief will get away with it and we'll lose Piotr.' There was no way she was going to lose Piotr without a fight.

Andrew obviously felt the same way. 'I don't even know where Poland is! It sounds like miles away.'

Snuggled in Piotr's arms, Kasia couldn't keep her eyes open. And she was getting heavy. 'I'm going to take her back upstairs, then we should make a plan.'

'Everything will feel better with a plan,' Minnie agreed.

* * *

As Piotr carried Kasia into the living room, Mum and Dad stopped talking. Mum was standing near the window. Dad was sitting on the sofa. The silence felt tense. Like the moment when a plane speeds up on the runway and everyone on board hopes it will fly.

'I'm going out,' Piotr said. 'With Minnie and Andrew. To the market.'

He laid the now-dozing Kasia on the sofa next to Dad.

'Don't stay out all day,' Dad said. 'There are arrangements to be made.'

Not if Piotr could help it, there weren't.

Piotr, Andrew and Minnie headed out of the flats, taking the shortcut that looped towards the market.

'What does your mum think?' Minnie asked.

Piotr shrugged. 'I don't know. She wants Dad to be happy, I suppose. They talked about it all last night.' He paused, remembering his parents' whispered voices . 'She misses Poland.'

It felt weird, thinking that his mum and dad had had a whole different life, in another country, before he was born. It felt like climbing and missing a rung on a ladder: it made his heart pound. That past was theirs, not his.

'Cake,' Andrew said, 'that's what you need.'

The cafe next to the salon was already busy. Market traders, finished with their set-up, queued for take-away tea. Early shoppers, keen for breakfast, were tucking into eggs and bacon. People on their way to work bought brown paper bags filled with sausage baps or bacon butties. The cafe smelled warm, cosy, tasty.

Piotr couldn't help wondering how many more times he'd be coming in here. Was this his last week in England? His second to last? He looked at the floor until the woozy feeling passed.

Minnie ordered and three drinks and three cakes were put on a tray. The booth in front of the big window was free, so they shuffled in. It was a while before any of them spoke. They were too busy with cake crumbs and cans.

Eventually, Andrew said, 'So, how are we going to save Piotr?'

'Well,' Minnie said, 'we need to, you know, find stuff out, investigate and things.' It had been her idea. She felt responsible for making it work. But even to her own ears, that answer sounded as sketchy as stick men.

'How, though? I don't know how to take fingerprints, or DNA or anything,' Andrew said.

Minnie bit her lip and looked out of the window.

She didn't have a clue where to begin and the cake had filled her stomach but left her brain unboosted.

'Hey!' Minnie leaned closer to the window. 'Hey, look!'

The other two craned their necks to see what she was pointing at. 'It's that girl! The rude one from the theatre.'

Sylvie, Piotr thought.

Sure enough, a girl with bright red hair and freckles was standing by the second-hand bookstall. Today she wore a purple backpack with key chains and badges decorating it. She was picking out titles carefully, cradling them while she read the back covers, then tucking them back on the shelves.

Piotr felt himself flush with anger.

Dad had already been feeling bad, before any of the necklace trouble had started. Because of this girl. It was partly her fault Dad wanted to leave the country.

'She can get us into the theatre!' Andrew said.

'She needs to learn some manners!' Minnie said.

There was a one-second pause, then all three of them slid out of the booth and out on to the street, heading straight for Sylvie.

She had turned away from the musty dustiness of the bookstall, towards the perfumed cloud of the florists.

'Hey!' Andrew shouted. 'Hey!'

The girl paused and looked around.

Andrew reached her first. 'We need to talk to you – you might be a witness.'

'You might be a witness,' Minnie added, 'but we also want to tell you you're very rude.'

Piotr didn't speak.

He watched as the girl's face went from confused, to surprised, to amused. She was actually smiling at them!

'It isn't funny,' Piotr said quietly. 'You were horrible to my dad at the theatre yesterday.'

The girl shook her head. 'No, I wasn't.'

'Yes, you were.'

'No,' the girl insisted. '*I* wasn't. But Sylvie probably was. Sylvie, my sister. My twin sister. I'm Flora.'

Twins?

Now that Piotr looked carefully at her, he could see that her eyes were a tiny bit softer than her sister's piercing blue ones. Flora's were more jabbing blue. And her cheeks were a tiny bit fuller. But unless you were looking really carefully, she could for all the world be the exact same girl.

'Twins?' Andrew said appreciatively. 'Cool!'

Minnie curled her top lip. 'There are two of you?'

Flora grinned. 'Not really. We look the same, but we're not the same. We're quite different. Sylvie, she likes to put on a show. I'm more … well … quiet.'

'That's good. The world couldn't handle two of her.' Minnie thrust out her hand. 'I'm Minnie. The daft one is Andrew. The tall one is Piotr.'

Piotr wasn't tall, not compared to Minnie, but he felt pleased anyway.

Andrew mostly ignored the insult, only scowling for a split second at Minnie.

Flora smiled shyly. 'Why are you looking for Sylvie?'

Andrew replied before either of the others had a chance. 'She's a witness. She might have seen the crime or the suspects. I guess she might even be the criminal herself. You could even be an accomplice!'

'I promise I'm not an accomplice to anything. I wouldn't know how to be. Mostly, I just read books and hang out.'

'Oh, OK. I don't think readers are criminals, are they?' Andrew looked at Minnie. She shrugged.

'Is it the diamond theft?' Flora asked.

'Yes. We're investigating,' Andrew replied. 'We're going to find the thief and stop Piotr here being sent to Poland.'

Flora looked confused. 'What's Poland got to do with the necklace?'

Piotr wasn't sure that he wanted Flora to know his business. She seemed nicer than her sister, but she was a stranger, after all.

Andrew didn't seem to notice Piotr's unease. 'They think Piotr's dad did it. He's the security guard. Mr Domek? And now, Mr Domek is so upset he's decided to take the whole family back to Poland. And we don't want Piotr to go.'

Flora's look of sympathy was real.

It made Piotr feel even worse. He didn't want strangers pitying him. He looked down at his scuffed trainers and wished the ground would swallow him up.

'So,' Andrew said, 'we need to ask Sylvie what she saw. It's the only way we'll get to keep Piotr. And we really, really want to keep Piotr.'

Flora smiled. 'You're investigators?' she asked. 'I love detective stories. They're my favourite. Can I help?'

'Yes,' Minnie replied. 'You can get your rude sister to talk to us.'

Flora bit her lip. 'I can try,' she said.

Chapter Six

'Why wouldn't Sylvie want to talk to us?' Andrew asked. 'We don't bite.'

Flora still looked worried. 'I can ask her, but, you see, she's not supposed to be disturbed while she's resting.'

Minnie rolled her eyes. Sylvie sounded like a proper precious princess.

'No, it isn't like that,' Flora said, catching the look. 'She's diabetic. Usually it's fine, but she has to be careful when her routine is messed up – like during rehearsals. Mum treats her like she's made of glass. Sylvie hates it, but she puts up with it.'

'Diabetic?' Andrew asked.

'It means that if she doesn't have enough sugar in her blood then she kind of faints. It doesn't happen very often, but when she's in a play she uses up more energy than normal. Mum can make a bit of a fuss.'

Minnie muttered a very quick 'sorry'. It was blink-and-you-miss-it quick. In the bustle of the market, with the traders calling out and the shoppers haggling back, it was likely that Flora hadn't heard Minnie's apology at all. But Minnie wasn't too bothered. Sylvie's problems didn't make Minnie feel sorry for her.

'So, she can't come out at all?' Andrew asked.

Flora shrugged. 'To be honest, just because Sylvie is told to do something doesn't mean she'll necessarily do it. I'll call her.'

She pulled out her phone and tapped quickly. In seconds, she was talking to Sylvie. '… There are some people who want to interview you,' Flora said. '… No, not press. Some investigators you met yesterday? They want to hear about the robbery from a first-hand perspective. We're near the cafe, around the corner from the theatre … Wait, I'll ask.' Flora looked up. 'She says she'll only talk to you if you buy her a cream cake.'

Piotr nodded helplessly. The girl was a nightmare.

'See you soon,' Flora said, then ended the call. 'Shall we go and wait in the cafe?'

The window booth still had their empty plates and half-drunk cans. So they sat back down and waited for Sylvie to appear. Flora asked how they knew one another.

Andrew explained about the blue paint. Andrew asked about being twins.

'It's nice, sometimes,' Flora said. 'But Sylvie's often busy – Mum too, with the play. So, I …' She waved at the market and the bookstall.

Piotr barely spoke. He was watching the street, looking for a telltale flash of red hair.

Then there she was! Arms swinging by her side, as though she were at the head of her very own marching band.

Piotr felt a rush of anger. He squished it down. Sylvie had information that might help keep him here. He had to keep his temper.

Minnie didn't feel the same way. She stood up and put her hands on her hips. She was a good head taller than Sylvie. But Sylvie, recognising the challenge, squared her shoulders too and looked Minnie right in the eye.

'You owe Piotr an apology,' Minnie said. 'Actually, you owe his dad one, but he isn't here, so Piotr will accept it on his behalf.' Andrew always made them watch the Oscar highlights, so she knew all about accepting things on other people's behalf.

'Why? An apology for what?' Sylvie said.

'Mr Domek. You were rude to him.'

Sylvie's face stayed blank.

'Mr Domek, who works on the stage door? Who you walk past all the time? Who made your ID badge?'

'Oh!' Sylvie said slowly. 'You mean the doorman? I wasn't rude. I was just getting my point across in the most efficient way.'

'It was rude.'

'I'm sorry you think that.'

'That's not an apology.'

'I'm sorry you think that too.'

'Neither was that!' Minnie was almost shouting. Around the cafe, people paused with cups held halfway to their mouths, or sausage rolls held in mid-air, and stared.

'It doesn't matter,' Piotr said roughly.

'It does!' Minnie said.

'Not for now, it doesn't. What matters now is that we find out what she knows. That's what will save Dad. Not some apology that she doesn't even mean.'

There was silence around the table. Then Minnie sat down and Sylvie slipped into the booth beside her.

'I'll have a custard tart,' Sylvie said.

'Don't push your luck,' Piotr warned.

'Fine. I'll be back in a second with a custard tart.' Sylvie slunk off to the counter.

'She's a nightmare,' Minnie said.

'She's not so bad when you get to know her,' Flora said. 'Honest.'

'She's our first lead,' Piotr said. 'We have to put up with her.'

Sylvie returned with a cake in foil casing balanced on a little white plate. She sat down serenely. She snapped off a tiny bit of the crust and nibbled at it glacially slowly.

Piotr forced himself to swallow his anger. It was difficult, but with clenched fists he managed to do it. 'We wondered if you could tell us what happened yesterday? The theft at the theatre?'

'Why?' Sylvie asked.

'Because it would really help us.'

'Why?'

'Because it would.'

Sylvie sniffed, wrinkling her nose as she did so. 'I don't know if I want to tell you.' She reached for a teaspoon and began to excavate tiny slivers of custard from the middle of her tart.

'Sylvie,' Flora said, 'they just want to hear the true story from someone who was really there, someone right in the middle of it. Someone with a totally individual and unique perspective.'

Sylvie licked the spoon and looked thoughtful. 'I suppose I *was* a key witness,' she said.

Piotr flashed Flora a grateful look; she really knew how to handle her sister. 'Can you tell us who was there?'

'Oh, hundreds of people,' Sylvie said.

Piotr's heart sank. Hundreds of suspects would take forever to track down. And he had no idea how long he had before Dad whisked them away.

'But, of course, most of them were on or around the stage when the theft took place.'

'How do you know when that was?' Andrew asked. He didn't mind too much what Sylvie was like. She was, more than anything, an actor, and that was good enough for Andrew.

And then she showed them why she deserved to be on the same stage as Betty Massino.

Sylvie closed her eyes for a second, paused, raised just the very tips of her fingers in a delicate gesture. They all leaned closer, despite themselves. Her eyes opened, and with a wicked grin, she said, 'It all started when Betty Massino died.'

Andrew gave a soft splutter.

'The actors were onstage, ready to read the final scene.

The house lights were off. We stood alone in gloomy darkness, like wraiths on a midnight moor.'

As Sylvie spoke, the bright sunshine of the cafe seemed to dim a little and night mists seemed to stroke the backs of their necks. She was an excellent actor.

'A spotlight came on, framing the desperate widow. Betty held her script, but her performance was breathtaking. She'd lost everything – home, help, hope ... all gone. She's invited to a feast. She hears the house will be torn down. She drips poison into a glass –' Sylvie mimed pouring a vial into a can. 'Drop by drop. She's carrying doom. Is the death meant for the new landlord? Or the widow herself?'

Andrew gasped. 'Who is it for?'

'She lifts a dagger from the table and plunges it into the landlord's heart. Then she gulps down the poison in one draught and falls to the floor. She means to kill them both! The spotlight snaps out. Betty is carried offstage ... The cast was weeping – even the crew was in tears. Everyone began talking about how wonderful Betty was, how amazing the play is going to be – that's how we know it wasn't any of us who stole the necklace, you see; we're all each other's alibis. And then the theatre echoed with the most terrible shrieks, coming from the principal dressing rooms. So, we all rushed to see what was the matter.' Sylvie took a breath and raised an eyebrow, keen to keep her audience waiting.

Minnie couldn't wait. 'Then what?'

'There she was, Betty Massino, standing over an open suitcase. She was screaming and crying and shouting for the police.' Sylvie said this as though it were the most amazing thing.

'Who else was there?' Andrew asked.

'Wait!' Piotr said. 'We should be taking notes. We might need to refer back to it later. Who's got a pen?'

Sylvie's spell was broken. The stage was gone, the cafe was back, with the clatter of cutlery on china, shouted orders, the smell of frying and baking and soapy washing up. They were back to earth with a bump. They looked at each other. It was the school holidays; no one was carrying notebooks or pencil cases.

Then Flora said shyly, 'I've got my phone. I could record it on there?'

Piotr nodded. 'Thank you.'

She pulled her phone from a side pocket and began voice recording.

'So,' Piotr asked, 'do you know when she last saw the necklace?'

Sylvie closed her eyes, as though trying to relive the scene. 'Betty told the police that she saw the necklace before we began reading the final scene at 6.15 p.m. We read for fifteen minutes. Most people were near the stage that whole time.'

Piotr propped his elbows on the tabletop. 'Who wasn't?'

Sylvie took another sliver of custard and licked the spoon.

Then she took another sliver.

Then another.

'Sylvie!' Piotr said.

'Well,' she said, 'let me think.' She snapped off more pastry and ate it agonisingly slowly.

'Sylvie!' Minnie snapped.

'Ooh, if you're going to shout, I won't help at all,' Sylvie said.

'I'm sorry. Minnie's sorry. Just, please, tell us.' Piotr held up his hands in defeat.

'Rumour has it – and theatre rumours are pretty good – rumour has it that there were four people who had time to slip into Betty's dressing room during those fifteen minutes. Wendy, the dresser, forgot her glasses and had to go up to wardrobe to get them. Nita, the stage manager, went to make a call. Albie, Betty's assistant, went to fetch a wrap for her in case she was cold on the floor. And, of course, the doorman, whatever his name is – he was never on the stage in the first place. Personally, I think he did it.'

Chapter Seven

Flora spoke before Minnie had a chance to do something she'd regret. 'The doorman is Mr Domek, Piotr's dad,' she reminded Sylvie.

Sylvie gave a small shrug in Piotr's direction, as if to say, 'Sorry, your dad's a thief.'

'He didn't do it,' Piotr said firmly. Sylvie was totally, absolutely and utterly a –

'What makes you so certain?' Sylvie interrupted his thought.

Dad. That's what made him so certain. But how could he possibly explain that to Sylvie? The way that Dad always expected him and Kasia to be the very best they could be. The way he worked long hours, into the night, to take care of the people he loved – Mum, Piotr, Kasia and their family back in Poland. The way he'd sleep on the floor of their rooms if they were ill, or sad, or frightened. There was no way this girl could understand all that.

Flora spoke again. 'Sylvie, he knows the same way we'd know if it were our dad.'

Sylvie pressed a fingertip into the foil container to gather every last crumb of pastry. She looked thoughtful. 'I guess it *could* have been one of the others,' she said finally. 'Now, I really have to go home, or Mum will be cross. Flora, do you want to come to the theatre later and mind my things?'

It didn't sound like a tempting offer to Piotr. It can't have seemed like one to Flora either. She shook her head. 'Your evidence is on my phone,' Flora explained. 'I need to write it down for Piotr.'

'I don't see why,' Sylvie sniffed. 'You three have no chance of finding the thief.'

'You four,' Flora corrected.

Piotr smiled. It seemed their gang had grown.

Sylvie left them moments later, with her nose in the air and out of joint. Flora grinned. 'Like I said, she likes the drama. She'll be fine.'

'What next?' Andrew asked.

'I'll go and buy a notebook,' Flora said. 'The bookseller out there had some blank ones. I can write down everything Sylvie said about the suspects. And we can record any clues we find. If that's OK?'

'You seem to know what you're doing,' Andrew said.

Flora smiled shyly. 'I want to be a forensic pathologist when I'm older. They examine dead bodies to work out how they died. I've got a book about it. Do you know, it's possible to tell where someone comes from just by studying the enamel on their teeth? Often teeth are the last thing to decompose.'

Andrew's mouth had dropped open. 'Wow,' he said.

'And coming back from Planet Yuck,' Minnie said, 'we'll need to interview the suspects like on TV.'

'And see the scene of the crime,' Flora added.

That seemed like a lot to Piotr. And none of it easy. 'How are we going to get the suspects to talk? And how will we get into the dressing room of a recently burgled Hollywood star?'

Piotr tapped his toes together as though he might be able to dislodge an idea from his feet.

Minnie wriggled. She squirmed. Then she gave a small *squee*. 'I've got it!' she said. 'I know how we'll get into the scene of the crime.'

'How?' Andrew asked.

Minnie looked at Flora.

Flora looked back.

Minnie looked harder.

Flora frowned. 'No.'

Minnie looked even harder.

'What?' Andrew asked.

'No way.' Flora shook her head.

Piotr realised what Minnie was thinking. He felt a tiny flare of excitement.

'Minnie,' Piotr said, 'you're brilliant!'

'What are you all talking about?' Andrew snapped.

Flora shook her head again, more firmly. 'I am not going to impersonate Sylvie to sneak us all into the theatre. What if we get caught? What if Sylvie finds out? What if Betty realises I'm not Sylvie and calls the police?'

'What if you don't do it and Piotr ends up living on the other side of the world?' Minnie asked.

'Poland isn't the other side of the world,' Flora replied crossly.

'Please?' Piotr asked.

'Pretty please with pink bows on?' Andrew added.

Flora gave a heavy sigh. 'Fine. But if we get caught I'm saying it's all your fault.'

'Yes!' Andrew said, thumping the air.

* * *

Outside the stage door, Flora looked paler than usual. Perhaps even a touch green. 'I feel sick,' she said.

'Don't worry, you can do this,' Minnie said. 'Didn't you ever pretend to be each other when you were little?'

'Yes. To confuse our ballet teacher, or to see if Mum could tell us apart! Never to gain illegal access to a celebrity crime scene!'

Andrew drew closer to look at her pupils. 'If you're having a panic attack, you should breathe into a paper bag. Do you want me to see if I can find one? I think there's an old chip bag in that bin over there.'

Piotr edged Andrew and Minnie back. 'Give her a bit of space. And leave that bin alone. You don't have to do this, you know, Flora. We can find another way.'

She flashed him a grateful look. 'No, it's OK. I'll give it my best shot. Come on, let's do this.'

She gave herself a quick shake, then walked through the stage door, her nose held high, as if the ground smelled bad.

The others followed a few steps behind, relying on Flora to get them in.

Piotr felt a sudden rush of emotion when he realised that the man sitting in Dad's chair behind the desk was a stranger. He was younger than Dad, thin, with blond hair.

'Can I help you?' the man said doubtfully.

Flora lifted her chin even further and gave a small sniff. Piotr had to stop himself from grinning – she had Sylvie down to a T.

'You're new,' Flora stated.

'Yeah, I'm Dave. I was sent from the agency this morning. It's just temporary, like, until they find someone permanent.'

'Fascinating,' Flora said with a long sigh. Then she walked towards the theatre door.

'Hey,' Dave said. 'Wait! You can't go through there.'

'I'm Sylvie Hampshire. I think you'll find I can.'

Dave flushed, then hurriedly dug out a piece of paper and drew his finger down it, looking for Sylvie's name. 'Oh, yes. You're on the list. I guess you can go through. But, what about the rest of you?'

Flora raised an eyebrow, her eyes as sharp as steel pins. 'My friends always come with me. Don't you know that?'

Dave looked at his list again. 'There's nothing … I mean, it doesn't say …'

'You'll learn,' Flora said. '*If* you're here for long enough. Come on!'

With that, she pushed open the black theatre door

and waltzed through. The others scooted in behind her, before the man on the desk had a chance to speak.

As soon as the door closed, Flora collapsed against the wall. 'Argh! That was awful. Terrible. I was so rude to him! Poor man. Should I go and apologise?'

'No!' the others said.

'You were great.' Minnie put a hand on Flora's shoulder and gave it a small squeeze. 'Totally brilliant. You got us in. Acting obviously runs in the family.'

Flora gave a small smile. 'Thanks.'

'Right,' Piotr said. 'We might get rumbled any minute. Let's find Betty Massino's dressing room.'

Piotr had heard Dad talk occasionally about the theatre. He would never have gossiped – he didn't approve of gossip – but one time he mentioned an actor needing a piano carrying up two flights of steps to his dressing room, and another who'd had so many deliveries of good-luck bouquets that Dad reckoned he'd climbed the equivalent of the Matterhorn delivering them.

So Piotr assumed the star dressing rooms were at the top of the building.

'We need to go up,' Piotr whispered.

They ignored a sign that pointed left to 'stage' and

instead found a staircase. They climbed, their footsteps echoing up the stairwell.

'Shh,' Piotr warned.

They tried to be quiet, but four people in a stairwell couldn't help but make a noise.

On the first landing, a huge number 1 was painted on the wall, and beside it was written *AV, company dressing rooms*.

'Is this it?' Andrew hissed.

Flora shook her head. 'Company means the regular cast members. Sylvie is company. Betty Massino's dressing room won't be with those.'

A sudden voice came from the corridor beyond the landing. '… And then she said to Derek it was the worst script she'd seen since playing the donkey in the school Nativity.'

A second voice roared with laughter.

The voices were headed towards the staircase!

'Up, up!' Piotr said. They raced, on tiptoe, up the stairs, away from the voices. They reached the next landing. Piotr waved for them all to freeze. They stood, statue-still, with pounding hearts, and listened. The voices headed away from them, down towards the stage. Piotr gave a silent sigh. He looked at the wall. It was labelled *2: wardrobe, principal dressing rooms*.

'Here,' Piotr said.

'Why does a wardrobe have its own sign?' Minnie whispered. 'Is it important, like the one that leads to Narnia?'

Flora giggled softly. 'It means the clothes that the theatre owns. There are probably hundreds and hundreds of outfits there. More like a costume shop than a regular wardrobe.'

'Wow.' Minnie gave an appreciative whistle.

'Shh,' Piotr tried again. They had to keep a low profile. Flora looked guilty. At least she was listening to him.

They found themselves in a gloomy corridor, lit by green running-man signs and ugly strip lights. There was no decoration, or carpet, or anything other than battleship-grey walls. Piotr was a bit disappointed. He'd imagined a theatre would be all red velvet and gold paint, like a sultan's palace. This was more sultan's prison.

He led the way along the corridor, reading the names on each of the doors. The corridor smelled of dust and a bit like the inside of Mum's make-up bag.

'Betty Massino' he read on the second door on the left. They had reached the scene of the crime.

Piotr turned the handle. The door didn't move.

He rattled the door. Locked.

He *almost* growled at it – they'd got inside the theatre and now one plank of stupid wood was keeping them out of the crime scene. But he didn't growl. Doing animal impressions wasn't really keeping a low profile either.

'What do we do now?' Andrew whispered.

'Well,' Flora said, 'I've got an idea.' She reached into her backpack and pulled out her library card.

'Books won't help,' Minnie said.

'Won't they?' Flora asked with a grin. 'I've never done this before, but I've read about it.' She held the door handle and squeezed her library card into the narrow space between the door and its frame. She jiggled it for a moment, trying to find the latch. Then, when Flora gave a sharp push with her library card, the door opened.

'Wow,' Andrew said. 'That's incredible.'

He was talking about Flora, not the dressing room. The dressing room was a bit of a disappointment.

Piotr stepped in first.

The room was small, like a broom cupboard with an en suite. It was about as glamorous as a broom cupboard too. There was a mirror, surrounded by a run of bulbs, that was true, but the paint around it was peeling in scabs. There was a rickety-looking chair in front of the mirror and a dressing table, its white plastic top curling up at the edges.

There was a clothes rail, with a black dress on a hanger. Beside that was a tiny shower cubicle and sink. Water dripped from the shower head into the tray; a nasty, tea-coloured stain on the tray suggested it had been dripping for a long time.

There wasn't really enough room for them all to fit inside.

'Well,' Minnie said in disappointment, 'this isn't Hollywood. More *Hollyoaks*.'

'Still,' Andrew said, reaching out to touch the dress on the hanger, 'that's Betty Massino's costume right there. That's what she wears onstage. And that's Betty Massino's make-up. And that's Betty Massino's tatty mirror. And that's the dagger Betty Massino uses to stab the landlord. And those are Betty Massino's good-luck cards!' He pointed to a row of greetings cards pinned above the mirror.

Piotr followed Andrew's gaze. There were lots of cards straddling a piece of string.

'Everyone, look for clues,' Piotr instructed.

The space was cramped as each of them looked. No one was sure what they were looking for, perhaps a lost button, a telling receipt, or a stray hair that would crack the case. Andrew was mostly just looking at the things Betty must have touched.

Piotr's eyes strayed back to the good-luck cards. Most had flowers or puppies or kittens on the front. But one was different. It had a black background with a white silhouette of a woman wearing jewels. He reached up and eased the card open.

Looking forward to watching you 'Sparkle'.
Your biggest fan, Philip.

It was perhaps meant to sound romantic, but it seemed a bit odd to Piotr. He took the card down. The handwriting was neat and precise, as though done with a ruler.

'Sylvie!' a voice roared from the doorway. 'What in tarnation is going on here?'

Flora's head whipped around. As did everyone else's. There was a tall, well-dressed man standing in the doorway, glaring at them all. He looked vaguely familiar.

'Sylvie? I asked you a question.' He spoke with an American accent.

Of course! This must be Albie, Betty's assistant.

Flora must have realised too. 'Sorry, Albie. I didn't mean any harm.'

'That's Mr Sandbaum to you, missy. Now, get out of

this dressing room before I have you kicked off this production.'

They needed no second telling. The four dashed past the angry assistant faster than he could say 'security'.

It was only when they crashed through an emergency exit sign and found themselves out on the street that Piotr realised he was still holding the weird-looking good-luck card. He slipped it into his back pocket, next to Jimmy's card.

He'd accidentally stolen from Betty Massino!

Chapter Eight

Should he tell the others about the card?

Piotr felt his face flush. They were trying to prove his dad's innocence. And he had just stolen from the exact same victim. He couldn't tell the others. Maybe Andrew and Minnie would be OK, but Flora … She had only just met him and yet she seemed to trust him. He couldn't betray that trust. He'd just keep it safe and try to find a chance to put it back.

Outside the emergency exit, Andrew was whooping with nervous laughter. Minnie held her hands to her chest, pressing down on her thumping heart. Flora looked queasy again.

'Did anyone find any clues?' Minnie asked.

Everyone shook their heads. Then Flora held up her phone. 'I filmed it, though, on my phone. So, if we need to check anything later, we can. I'll print some pictures for my notebook too.'

They strolled back through the square, towards Marsh Road.

'I'd better get home,' Piotr said. 'Will we meet tomorrow?' The others agreed and they said goodbye – Piotr didn't mention the card in his pocket.

He walked back slowly. They'd seen the crime scene, but they were no closer to finding the real jewel thief.

Which meant he was getting closer to living in Poland.

Mum would be expecting him home soon. But he found himself dawdling. Here, by himself, in the old familiar town, it almost felt as if he were seeing things for the very first time – the way that broken paving stones were circled, like spelling mistakes, in yellow spray paint; the way that lamp posts had metal shields clutched to their fronts; the way the lime-green bramble fruit swelled like plague pustules between railings.

This was home.

Here.

He couldn't imagine living anywhere else.

He didn't want to imagine it.

At the flat, Kasia was sitting on the sofa in front of CBeebies. Her mouth hung open as she stared at the pink and blue and green dancing characters on TV. She giggled when he tickled her tummy, but her eyes didn't leave the screen.

Piotr wandered into the galley kitchen. It was a small space and today it was made even smaller by a pile of flattened cardboard boxes leaning up against the cooker. Mum was wrapping plates in newspaper.

'What's going on? You're not packing already?' he asked.

'No,' Mum said. 'Not yet. But I thought even if we stay, we need a good clear-out. These are for the charity shop. Are you hungry?' she added.

'Mmm.' Piotr opened the fridge, picked out a slice of ham and rolled it into a tube. He popped the whole tube in his mouth.

'Hey!' Mum flicked his wrist lightly. 'I'll make you something.' She took out bread and one of the big tomatoes she liked to buy from Polski Sklep.

'Where's Dad?'

Mum passed him a lettuce. 'Wash that, would you?' she asked.

Piotr tugged the leaves, snapping the stems, and dropped the leaves into a colander. 'Where's Dad?' he asked again as he rinsed them under the cold tap, realising that Mum hadn't answered him.

She sighed. 'Out.'

Piotr suddenly felt cold. Mum didn't usually talk in riddles. She said exactly what she thought and no more. He turned off the tap and looked at her.

Her cheeks were red. She held the backs of her hands against them.

'Mum?' Piotr asked warily. 'What's going on?'

'He's gone to see Janek. He heard Jan's uncle has a house to rent in Gdansk.'

'Gdansk?' Piotr knew that was a big city in Poland. 'Why does Dad care about a house in Gdansk?'

'He's thinking about renting it for us, Pietrucha.'

'But I don't want to go to Gdansk!'

Mum paused at the chopping board. 'I know,' she said quietly. 'But you must understand how difficult it is here now. Your father, he's –' she searched for the right word, her face creased with worry – 'he's a very proud man. You know that. This country, it hasn't always been good to us. And now, well, it's the last straw.'

Mum kept her eyes down. Piotr suddenly worried that there might be tears there, waiting to fall.

'We came here with a lot of hope. We were going to work hard, send money home. We thought we'd go back to have you. But you can't plan life. We never did go back. And it's hard to be in a country you don't properly understand.'

'But you've learned English.'

Mum nodded slowly. 'Yes, but when I speak in English, it feels as though I'm running a car with a rusty engine. I have to think before I speak. And the people at work think I have no sense of humour because I never get the jokes. Dad just wants to be back in a place where they understand what he is. Where hard work counts. Where people trust each other. You'll soon settle in there. You're Polish too.'

Piotr didn't reply. He couldn't.

How could he explain that English and Polish were both in his head, side by side? No, not even side by side. They were one language. Just in the way he used one type of English with his friends, and another with his teachers, Polish was just the English he used at home.

He didn't want his world to be boring – to shrink to just one word for potato, or sister, or tree.

Or friend.

Piotr heard a key turn in the door. Kasia squealed from next door as Dad walked in.

Then Dad was at the kitchen door. He smiled at them both.

'How did it go?' Mum asked.

'Good. Excellent. It sounds like a good house, a good part of town. We shouldn't wait – we should take it.'

Mum lifted a heavy dish into the cardboard box. 'So soon?' she said quietly. 'What about the police, Pawel?'

'The police are doing nothing. They know nothing. They say it's "innocent until proven guilty", but what happens when nothing is proved? Am I to live under this suspicion forever? I can't do it, Magda. I can't.'

Piotr felt his stomach plummet right through his shoes and pool on to the kitchen floor.

Mum frowned too. 'If you're serious, we need to find a school before the holidays are over. We need to find work. A nursery for Kasia.'

'We'll have family to help with the children. Work will be easy. We're not going back to the Poland we left.'

'It would be nice to be near my sisters,' Mum said softly.

'No!' Piotr shouted. 'I don't want to.'

Dad shook his head. 'We'll go at the weekend to visit our family. To talk to your cousins about their school. We'll visit the house in Gdansk. You'll like it, you'll see. You might even stay for the rest of the holiday, while we pack up here.'

Piotr couldn't speak. It was all happening too quickly.

'Magda,' Dad said. 'We're going home.' He said the word 'home' as though he were settling into a warm bath.

Mum reached out and wrapped her arms around Dad. 'If you're sure that's what you want.'

Piotr gripped the sink tightly.

He might have only four days left in the place that had always been home.

Four days to solve the crime and save himself.

And he had no idea how he was going to do it.

Chapter Nine

Piotr waited until Mum was bathing Kasia. Dad was on his own, washing up after tea. Piotr silently picked up a tea towel and began wiping the dishes.

There was plenty of space in the cupboards now that Mum had packed so much for the charity shop.

Dad dried his hands on the front of his jeans and flicked on the radio. Mum had left it on a pop station, so Dad retuned it to classical.

Piotr realised Dad wasn't going to say anything. If they were to talk, it was up to him. 'Dad, I don't want to leave.'

Dad paused, then said, 'I know, I do. But it's for the best.'

'It isn't fair. You and Mum won't listen to me.'

'Fair? And is it fair that I am suspended from work? And the police are doing nothing?'

'Why don't you give the police a chance to solve the crime before leaving?'

'I don't want to talk about the police, or the theft. I just want us to look forward to the future now, Piotrek.'

'But if we go, they might think you're running away!'

Dad started. He looked as though he'd been slapped. 'They wouldn't think that. They couldn't.'

'They might.'

'Then they are even bigger fools than I thought. Who are they to judge me? Without a shred of evidence. What kind of a place is this, where the police decide what to think before investigating?'

Piotr didn't know how to answer. He dried a mug and hung it from a hook. 'Who do you think did it?'

Dad didn't reply.

'You must have an idea,' Piotr tried again.

'Why? Because I was responsible for security?'

'No!' It wasn't Dad's job to protect everyone, that was impossible. 'No, just because you were there. I thought you might have seen something.'

'I … I wasn't …' Dad stopped abruptly. He plunged his hands back into the soapy water and began scrubbing at a pan.

'What?'

'Nothing. I really don't want to discuss this any more.'

Piotr frowned at Dad's back. What had he been going to say? Dad wasn't what?

'You must be looking forward to seeing your cousins and your aunts at the weekend?'

Dad was changing the subject. Badly.

As Piotr took a pan and began to wipe off the drips, he couldn't help but wonder, what was Dad not saying?

Chapter Ten

The gang met the following morning, at the cafe. They sat in a brittle silence as Piotr told them about the plan to check out Gdansk.

'Well, we need to be a bit more systematic,' Flora said once Piotr had finished. 'In the detective books I read, there's always a system.'

Piotr wriggled on the bench. He wasn't much of a reader. Or a detective. 'What kind of a system?'

Flora grinned. Her freckled nose creased with pleasure. She reached into her backpack and pulled out a notebook. 'I wrote down everything we found out yesterday – who was around at the right time, the layout of the building, the clues. Not that we have any clues. And I glued in pictures.' Her notebook looked like a school project. She'd even decorated the cover with pictures of magnifying glasses and a weird hat.

'What's that?' Andrew asked, pointing at the weird hat.

'A deerstalker. Sherlock Holmes wears one.'

'I didn't know we needed uniforms,' Andrew said.

'You must have spent all night on that,' Minnie said in wonder.

Flora shrugged. 'Mum was helping Sylvie with her lines. I was kind of by myself. And anyway, I liked doing it. I think next we should interview our suspects.'

'I want to as well,' a voice said.

Piotr looked up. Sylvie was standing at the end of the booth. She had a determined expression on her face.

'No way,' Minnie said.

'But I can help.'

'Why do you want to?' Piotr asked. He could think of no reason why Sylvie would want to be part of their gang.

'Because Flora's doing it,' Sylvie said. 'We do everything together.'

'No, you don't,' Minnie snapped. 'You go onstage without her.'

'Apart from that,' Sylvie said, 'we do everything together.'

Flora gave a twitchy smile. 'And school. She goes to stage school.'

'Apart from the play and school, we do everything together.'

Flora grinned wider. 'And ballet. I gave that up. And you don't come to Brownies, or with me and Dad when he takes me for a hot chocolate on Saturday mornings.'

Sylvie caught her sister's eye. They both grinned identical grins. 'I want to join your gang,' Sylvie said, 'because my sister and I *never* do *anything* together and I miss her. Also because everyone at the theatre is nervous and grumpy and I don't like it there now. I want to fix it.'

Minnie frowned. 'Well, you can't.'

Sylvie gave a haughty sniff and sat down. She almost landed on Andrew's lap – he had to shuffle out of the way.

Piotr knew Minnie was probably right. Sylvie was spoiled and bossy and could flounce off in a huff at any minute. But she did have access to the theatre, which might be very useful indeed.

'All right, then ... on one condition,' he said.

Sylvie made her own little huffing sound. 'What?'

'I want a proper apology for my dad.'

'If I help get to the suspects and find the necklace and clear his name and keep you in town and save the day, will that be a proper apology?'

Piotr paused. 'I suppose. But you're not in charge. OK?'

Sylvie gave a tight smile. 'Fine. So, what's the plan, boss?'

Piotr felt his hands get a bit sweaty. He didn't have a plan.

Sylvie was staring at him.

How was he suddenly in charge of four investigators? He didn't know the first thing about investigating. Or the second thing, or any of the hundred things you probably had to know. He hadn't asked to be in charge.

Sylvie was still staring at him.

Then he felt something being pushed into his open fingers. Flora's notebook. He gave her a quick 'thank you' smile.

He flipped open the notebook and looked at her neat list of suspects. 'What we need to do,' he said, 'is interview everyone on this list. We'll split up so that we can cover more ground. We've only got until Saturday to crack this case before I'm Gdansked for good.'

Chapter Eleven

Flora's list looked like this:

Wendy Williams – dresser and wardrobe mistress
Nita Khan – props and stage manager
Albie Sandbaum – Betty's assistant

Then, in teeny, tiny letters at the bottom:

Pawel Domek – stage-door security (sorry, Piotr!!!)

Piotr decided not to say anything about that last name on the list; after all, his attempt to talk to Dad had been a disaster … 'So, there are three interviews we need to do,' he said.

'Four,' Sylvie said, leaning across the table and pointing at Dad's name with a dainty finger. 'You shouldn't ignore any leads. Especially not leads you live with. He might have seen something.'

Piotr just grunted in reply. He felt his face redden. He hadn't told the others about the good-luck card he'd taken, and now he wasn't telling them about Dad being secretive. He was already being a bad leader.

They were all looking at him. He coughed.

'Well?' Sylvie asked.

The leads. They had to follow the leads.

'We split up,' Piotr said. 'It will be easier for one or two of us to chat to the suspects. If we go in a big gang, they'll only think we're trying to mug them or something.'

'Fine, but we want to work together!' Sylvie said, gesturing at her sister.

'No, it might come in useful later, you two being twins,' Piotr said. It had been useful at the theatre yesterday, and Sylvie couldn't have everything her own way.

'But Flora's been to the theatre loads. Most of them have seen her,' Sylvie said with a pout.

'Well, let's not remind them.'

'The element of surprise!' Andrew said.

'Considering that we are five kids with no experience, no training and not much of a clue what we're doing,' Minnie said, 'I imagine we've got the element of surprise.'

'I can get us into the theatre,' Sylvie said proudly.

'Is that the best place to find the suspects?' Andrew asked.

Sylvie thought for a moment, screwing up her mouth. 'Hmm. Wendy always brings in her lunch and eats in wardrobe. But Albie and Nita go out – I don't know where to.'

'We'll follow them!' Andrew said with a grin. 'In disguise!'

'Why do we need disguises?' Flora asked.

'Why not?' Andrew said. 'Everything's better in disguise.'

Piotr closed the notebook and handed it back to Flora. 'It will have to be Sylvie to interview Wendy, as she can get into the theatre easiest. One of us should go with her to help.'

Piotr looked at Andrew and Minnie.

Minnie rolled her eyes, but then she said, 'I'll go. Andrew would just spend the whole time looking out for famous people and wouldn't get any work done.'

'Hey!' Andrew said crossly.

'Your last school report said, "needs to focus" – and you know it did,' Minnie said.

Andrew shrugged. It had.

'Thanks, Minnie,' Piotr said. 'Flora and I will talk to Nita. Andrew, you've got Albie. OK?'

'How will we make her talk?' Flora asked nervously, her cheeks flushed pink.

'I don't know exactly,' Piotr said. 'I've never been a detective before either. I think you should just be nice. Be yourself.'

'But in disguise,' Andrew added with a grin.

Chapter Twelve

Minnie and Sylvie left the cafe first.

Outside, Marsh Road was busy. The sun was high, toasting the market. It felt warm on Minnie's skin. Sylvie walked like there was no one else on the street. Though Minnie was taller than Sylvie, she still had to stride to keep up. It was too hot for running, Minnie thought crossly.

'You should get out of the way for old people and people with prams and shopping and things,' Minnie said.

Sylvie didn't reply.

Minnie felt herself bristle. 'Why are you helping us? What's in it for you?'

Sylvie sighed. 'You simply wouldn't understand.'

Minnie clamped her mouth shut to stop herself saying something rude.

'None of you understand. We've been rehearsing for

weeks now. I mean the company. Betty Massino didn't have time in her schedule to start at the same time as us. She's catching up. But the cast have been working together for ages – we're like a big family. So, to think that someone at the theatre would steal, it's just horrible.'

Minnie was surprised. She hadn't thought that Sylvie could care about anything other than herself. Though, perhaps technically, worrying about the theatre not being fun was still thinking about herself. 'You want it to be the same as it was before?'

Sylvie nodded. 'I felt like I fitted in. I was part of something. And now I'm not.'

Minnie looked at the neat, white girl, with her nice clothes and exciting job. 'If you feel left out, then there's no hope for the rest of us.'

'I told you you wouldn't understand,' Sylvie said huffily.

'I think I understand you fine.'

'No, I'm full of surprises,' Sylvie said with a grin.

They'd reached the theatre and the stage door.

Sylvie went inside as though she belonged there. Which Minnie supposed she did. She walked up to the desk, where Dave was sitting. Sylvie turned to Minnie, arched an eyebrow and then turned back to the security guard.

'Hello, Dave,' Sylvie said. 'I wonder if you might help me, please?'

Dave looked a little startled.

Minnie felt a bit startled too. Was she watching Sylvie *trying to be nice*?

'I was hoping,' Sylvie continued, 'that I might be able to bring a friend in today. Would that be OK with you? Please?'

Dave nodded. 'Sure. I found out that there *is* a proper system, as it happens. You just need to sign her into the visitors' book. Here.' He handed Sylvie a pen.

As she signed, Dave gave a satisfied nod. 'That wasn't hard, was it?' he said. 'Not like yesterday.'

Minnie took her badge quickly, before Sylvie had a chance to ask Dave what he was talking about.

Moments later, Minnie was on the theatre side of the lobby, all official, with the badge on a string around her neck, the word *VISITOR* printed on it in black ink.

She'd been allowed in. Properly. With no hiding in stairwells. 'Thanks,' she muttered.

Sylvie gave a wide smile. 'You're welcome,' she sang, heading for the stairs. 'Wardrobe is this way.'

Minnie didn't have the heart to tell Sylvie that she knew. She didn't want to get Flora into trouble, after all.

As they went past *1: AV, company dressing rooms,* Sylvie paused. 'AV is audiovisual. And *my* dressing room is down there. Actually, if we're going to visit wardrobe, we'll need an excuse. Wait here.' She dashed off and returned in moments carrying a grey dress. She took hold of the cuff and gave a small yank. A strip of pale lace ripped loose. 'Now we've got an excuse!'

On the next level up – *2: wardrobe, principal dressing rooms* – Sylvie led the way past Betty Massino's locked door, to a door marked *Wardrobe and prop store*.

They stood outside the door, looking at the handle.

'What's Wendy like?' Minnie asked.

'Er, OK. Ish,' Sylvie replied. 'A bit … grumpy.'

'How grumpy?'

'Think tiger with a head cold.'

'I thought you said you were all one big, happy family?'

'Yes, well, every family has skeletons in the closet. We've got a witch in the wardrobe.'

Sylvie reached out and opened the door.

The room inside was pitch-black. There were no windows and the lights were off.

'She's not here,' Sylvie said in surprise.

'Perfect! We can snoop first!' Minnie said.

'I don't know if that's a good idea. Like I say, grumpy.'

Minnie paused. Anyone Sylvie was scared of was probably pretty terrifying. 'Thirty seconds, that's all. I promise. No one will ever know we've been here. Please?'

Sylvie gave a grim nod.

They stepped into the room. The door closed silently behind them. Sylvie fumbled for the light switch.

As soon as she could see the space, Minnie gasped.

The room was huge. Absolutely enormous. The second thing Minnie noticed was that it was piled high with objects. It was a treasure trove of *things*: vases, candlesticks, typewriters, swords, paintings, fake fruit, stuffed birds, radios. The nearest set of shelves was piled with stuff, every item tagged and arranged like a museum.

Beyond the shelves, the *clothes*! Long racks stretched into the distance, each full of costumes with neat labels hanging from their sleeves.

'It smells funny,' Minnie said, not wanting to show Sylvie how impressed she was. 'It smells like charity shops.'

Sylvie ignored her.

Minnie walked further into the room. Here the shelves on the left were arranged with plastic tubs, labelled things like *bracelets 1920s* or *earrings 1880s*.

On the right was a display of hats. Minnie took out her phone and snapped a few photos of a deerstalker for

Flora. Then she leaned in closer. It didn't smell of charity shops here. It smelled of something much closer to home. Varnish? She moved aside a top hat. Tucked behind it was a bottle of plum-black nail varnish with the lid not screwed on properly.

'Is it a clue?' Sylvie asked. 'It isn't labelled. All the props are labelled. If it's just ordinary make-up, then it definitely shouldn't be in here. Wendy is precious about people not getting stains on their costumes. That would definitely stain.'

Minnie couldn't help feeling a bit irritated by Sylvie's enthusiasm. Piotr wasn't Sylvie's friend; this wasn't her business, not really. 'Look at this place,' Minnie said. 'Is that stuffed fox head a clue? What about that box of umbrellas? Or that plastic lobster?' She took a photo of the nail varnish – just in case – then put the top hat firmly back where she'd found it.

They wandered further into the room. Minnie was amazed by how carefully everything was arranged – it could easily have looked like a jumble sale, but everything was too neatly ordered.

'I wish we could try on some of the costumes,' Minnie said wistfully. She thought she could see a fairy godmother dress and a suit of armour tucked in the shadows.

'Wendy would eat you alive,' Sylvie said.

'Too right she would,' a voice said from behind them. The door was open and a woman stood blocking the exit.

'Hello, Wendy,' Sylvie said in her most sunshiny voice.

'I'll give you hello. Breathing all over everything and disturbing my sequins. Who's this? Why is she in my wardrobe?'

Wendy shuffled into the room and glared at Minnie. She was old. Minnie couldn't guess her age, but her face was a map of wrinkles and her hair was grey and white. Her eyes were a sharp green. She looked like a bad-tempered seagull.

'This is my friend, Minnie,' Sylvie began.

'And what is your friend Minnie doing in here, upsetting everything?'

Minnie was about to argue – she hadn't touched anything, expect for a poxy top hat and she'd put it right back where she'd found it.

Sylvie shot her a warning look.

Minnie swallowed her words. Wendy probably wasn't someone to disagree with, even if she was wrong.

Sylvie handed over her costume. 'It's the cuff. It tore.'

Wendy took the dress and tutted at the sleeve.

She moved towards the back of the room. Now Minnie

noticed a desk, or workbench, slotted between two rows of shelves. Everything on the wooden bench was meticulously arranged. Measuring tape, scissors, pins and pincushion all aligned perfectly. A complicated sewing machine, like a mechanical torture device, was set up in pride of place. Beside the bench was a headless mannequin wearing a long, black dress and a loop of jet-black beads around its severed neck. A bowl of black sequins shone like beetles beside the machine.

From a drawer, Wendy took out a pair of glasses and stared at the torn sleeve.

'Tear, did it? All by itself? Or were you doing something stupid? Wouldn't put it past you.'

Sylvie didn't argue, she just said 'sorry' in a quiet voice.

Wendy put down Sylvie's dress. 'I'll fix your dress later, Sylvie Hampshire. Though I should make you go onstage with it torn to teach you for being careless.'

She took up one of the black sequins and speared it with a needle.

Minnie saw an opportunity to get on Wendy's good side. 'Can I help you with those?'

Wendy looked at Minnie's dirty fingers and chewed fingernails with all the distaste of a duchess looking at a mud pie. 'I wouldn't let you touch Betty Massino's wardrobe if it were on fire and you were the fire brigade,' she said. 'This silk is imported especially. This stitching is all hand-sewn. This dress is practically couture. Which means your mucky mitts are going nowhere near it.'

Oh.

Wendy hadn't finished complaining. 'Sylvie, you look taller. Don't tell me you've grown again. I can't let the hem down any more.'

Sylvie's voice shook a tiny, teeny touch as she replied, 'No, I haven't grown, I promise.'

Minnie was quite enjoying the effect Wendy was having on Sylvie. It was like seeing a spitting cat come face to face with an angry tiger. But they hadn't come here to get told off. Minnie remembered Piotr – he was relying on them.

Minnie cleared her throat. 'It was awful about the theft, wasn't it?' she said.

Wendy looked at Minnie sharply.

'Little girl, I have a hundred sequins to sew on to Betty Massino's dress before I go home tonight. If you think I have time to chit-chat with you, you are very much mistaken. Not when this fool has torn her costume and made extra work for me.'

Sylvie seemed to shrink into her shoes. Even Minnie's toes curled a little. The dresser *was* a witch.

'I was just interested,' Minnie whispered. 'I know Mr Domek a little bit.'

'Well, curiosity killed the cat. I told the police everything I know and that's the end of it. It's not my concern if Pawel lost his job over it. He shouldn't have been away from his desk – even if he had nothing to do with the theft. He should stay on stage door, where he belongs.'

'You saw Mr Domek?' Minnie gasped.

'Near enough. I was going up to get my glasses and I saw the back of his head in the lower corridor, scuttling towards the company dressing rooms. He must have heard me coming up while he was on his way down, so he pegged it.'

Wow. Minnie could hardly think straight. It was Wendy who had reported seeing Mr Domek at the scene of the crime. It was Wendy who had put the police on to Piotr's dad as the main suspect. It was Wendy's fault that Piotr was going away.

But she had only reported what she'd seen. Would she have any reason to lie?

'There are too many people in places they shouldn't be, if you ask me,' Wendy said.

'You mean us?' Sylvie asked tentatively.

'You and everyone else. That Nita hasn't given me a proper explanation of why my 1870s hairpins were on the wrong shelf. It must have been her. She can't get it into her head that accessories aren't props – they're wardrobe: *my* department. She's no business touching them. But she won't apologise. And until she does, she's not welcome in here.'

'Do you think Mr Domek stole the necklace?' Sylvie asked.

'Wouldn't put it past him.'

Minnie could feel the anger build up inside her like the jet in a water cannon. This stupid, mean woman had just made her mind up and that was that. And she went around saying anything she liked with no evidence.

Minnie swivelled on her heel. She wasn't listening to one more minute of this rubbish.

She was all set to storm out when something made her pause.

On the shelves behind Wendy's desk was a photo in a frame. It was tucked into a space between the rows of folders and catalogues and reference books.

It was a photo of Wendy with her arm around a man.

And it was a man that Minnie recognised.

It was a man who made her suddenly feel very frightened.

She still had the camera open on her phone. She snapped quickly.

'What on earth do you think you're doing?' Wendy gasped.

'Nothing! We have to go,' Minnie said, grabbing Sylvie's arm.

'What?' Sylvie sounded confused. 'What's the matter?'

Minnie tugged Sylvie towards the door, barrelled her through and then slammed it shut behind them. Minnie closed her eyes and tried to breathe slowly. To think.

'And what were you two doing, stepping into the lion's den?' a soft, American voice said.

Minnie opened her eyes.

Standing there, not a metre away, was Betty Massino.

Chapter Thirteen

Piotr, Andrew and Flora were on a stake-out. They'd left the cafe a few minutes after Minnie and Sylvie. They were headed to the theatre to follow Nita and Albie.

'I'm not doing it without a disguise,' Andrew said. 'Albie threw us out of Betty's dressing room. He might recognise me and blow my cover.'

Flora grinned. 'You haven't got a cover to blow.'

'I will once I have a disguise.'

They were walking through the market. Andrew paused by the fruit stall. No, attaching bananas to his jacket wouldn't be a good disguise. Albie might notice if he was trailed by a fruit salad.

'What you need,' Piotr said, 'is something to blend in with the crowd. Like a businessman reading the *Financial Times*, or a shopper with a plastic bag on each arm.'

'No,' Andrew said. 'I don't want to blend in. I want to stand out. I think I need to be a reporter. If he thinks I work for a newspaper, then he's more likely to talk, don't you think?'

Flora picked up an apple, paused and put it back down again. 'You need a notebook.'

'And some shades,' Andrew added.

They bought a ring-bound notebook from the bookseller, and a pen. A random knick-knack stall had some cheap sunglasses that covered half of Andrew's face. 'But I can't see without my glasses,' he said sadly, and put the sunglasses down. He smoothed back his hair and pulled up the collar on his polo shirt. 'Do I look older?'

Flora nodded. 'You look at least sixteen. You could be a junior reporter.'

'I could be Clark Kent! You're Lois Lane.' Andrew pointed at Flora. 'And you're Lex Luthor,' he told Piotr.

'I don't want to be the bad guy,' Piotr protested.

'And I want to be Superman,' Flora said.

'We can't all be Superman,' Andrew said, trying to slick back his hair.

'None of us is Superman.' Piotr was keen to get

Andrew back on track. 'We're investigators. I think you're a pretty convincing junior reporter.'

'Let's see if I can convince Albie,' Andrew said.

They found a bench across the road from the theatre with quite a good view down the alley to the stage door. It was nearly dinner time and theatre people were hurrying in the direction of sandwich shops or strolling into cafes.

'So, what does Nita look like?' Piotr asked Flora.

'She's Asian. Really petite. She had a scarf last time I saw her – oh, look, there she is now!'

A woman in a black tunic, which came down over wide, black trousers, was walking out of the stage door and turned towards the square. She had her head down; the loose scarf she wore meant they couldn't see her face very clearly.

'Are you sure?' Piotr asked.

'Yes,' Flora replied, 'stage managers always wear black. I think it's a rule. That's definitely Nita.'

Piotr turned to Andrew. 'We'll follow her. Do you mind waiting for Albie on your own?'

Andrew's eyes goggled. 'Are you joking? A chance to speak, by myself, to the assistant of one of the most famous people in the world? I think I'll cope.'

They left Andrew perched on the top of the bench, watching the stage door. Piotr and Flora followed Nita at what they hoped was a safe distance.

'Shouldn't we duck behind parked cars and things?' Flora asked.

'I think that might look a bit weird, don't you? I mean, how often do you see people in the street trying to hide behind lamp posts? It stands out a bit. I reckon if we just keep her in sight and don't get too close we'll be fine.'

Nita crossed the square and dawdled through the market, nodding a few hellos at stallholders. The street was busy, with families satelliting around pushchairs, shoppers laden with bags-for-life bulging with vegetables and new socks and novelty alarm clocks. It was easy to keep an eye on Nita without getting spotted.

Nita stopped for longest at the bargain sweet stall. She picked up bags of red laces and then a packet of flying saucers, then put them back. She dithered over a nougat bar.

Piotr and Flora edged closer.

They could hear Nita sighing now as she prodded a net full of chocolate coins. Finally, she picked up a Snickers and held it up to the stallholder.

'You sure?' he said with a sympathetic grin.

'I'm sure.' She handed over some coins, then slipped the chocolate into her handbag.

'Now?' Flora whispered.

'No, let's see what she does.'

Nita wandered past a few more stalls, but none seemed as interesting as the sweets. She looped back around the end of the market and walked towards the row of shops. She paused to look in the window of the cafe, but didn't go in. She passed Minnie's mum's salon without a glance, then headed into the junk shop.

It had boxes of old tools outside; low stools and chipped chairs were arranged on the pavement; jugs, vases and trays of cutlery were displayed in the window. It was hard to see inside past all the clutter. They waited for a second, to see if Nita reappeared, but she didn't, so they followed her in. The shop smelled of fusty, musty, old things – like a drawer that hasn't been opened for ages.

They saw Nita at the back of the shop, in the furniture section, sitting on a battered high-backed chair. She was so small and slight she looked lost in all the leather. Her feet barely touched the ground. She was leaning to one side, with her eyes closed. She held the unwrapped Snickers bar in front of her nose and sniffed at it hard.

They watched her for a minute. She seemed transported, as though she had forgotten that she was in a manky old junk shop and was instead on some Caribbean island with sand between her toes.

They edged closer.

Nita ignored them.

Piotr knew this was their chance. This was the moment when they could ask her about the robbery. This was their chance to discover whether she had stolen the necklace. He had to speak, he had to ask her something, something clever, something insightful. Flora was looking to him. Waiting.

'Are you going to eat that?' Piotr asked eventually.

He could have cried. Why had he said that? He was a terrible lead investigator.

Nita's eyes opened slowly. She frowned. 'No,' she said sadly. 'It's Ramadan. I won't be eating it until the sun sets. But smelling it is almost as good.'

Piotr wasn't sure that smelling a chocolate bar was anywhere near as good as eating it, but felt it would have been rude to say so.

Nita must have known what he was thinking, though. She sighed and held out the Snickers. 'Who'm I kidding? Do you want it? Even the comfiest chair and the waft of sugar aren't going to cheer me up. You might as well get the benefit.'

Nita glanced over at Flora. She gave a start of recognition. 'Sylvie?' she asked.

'No, I'm Flora – Sylvie's twin sister. We met once a few weeks ago at casting. I was my sister's "moral support".'

'Oh, yes. Well, I'm sure your friend will share the chocolate if you ask nicely.'

Piotr took the chocolate, broke it in half and handed a piece to Flora. They stood eating companionably.

'Is it good?' Nita asked wistfully. 'What's it like?'

'Mmm hmm,' Piotr mumbled between bites.

'It's lovely,' Flora said. 'Like splashing in a chocolate puddle.'

'Good. I'm glad.'

'Why do you need cheering up?' Flora asked.

'Work. Life.' Nita shrugged.

'Why? What's wrong? Thank you for the chocolate, by the way. It's delicious.'

'I shouldn't really gossip,' Nita said.

Flora gave a shy smile. 'I don't know if it's even possible to gossip with *children*. I mean, who are we going to tell? Sometimes talking about things can help, my dad says.'

'You're sweet,' Nita said.

'Can you tell us?' Flora said gently.

Piotr was impressed; Flora seemed to know exactly what to say.

'Well,' Nita said slowly, 'you'll think I'm being silly, but the theatre feels cursed right now. The theft was horrible. It wasn't just that Betty lost the necklace, it's that all the trust has gone. All this suspicion, it's like a sickness. A theatre company without trust is just terrible.'

Nita flopped back in the chair and curled her legs up under her. She looked like a child, though her face was tired and drawn. 'They stole more than a necklace; they stole the heart out of the company. Now there are rows all the time.'

Nita looked so sad. Piotr couldn't imagine for a second that Nita had had anything to do with the theft. In his mind, he drew a big black line through Nita's name on the suspect list.

Unless she was a brilliant actress.

'Who's rowing?' Flora asked.

Nita muttered something they didn't catch. Then, louder, 'As if I'd touch her stupid jewellery. Why would I? I know the difference between props and wardrobe. But she won't shut up about it.'

'Who?' Piotr asked.

Nita shook her head. 'I shouldn't get angry – it's not her fault. She's got enough on her plate with that waster brother of hers. I should be more forgiving, I know.'

She lapsed into silence and glowered.

Piotr and Flora exchanged a look. What plate? What brother?

Piotr wasn't sure what to ask next.

Flora leaped in. 'The police aren't any closer to finding the necklace, are they?' she asked.

Nita shook her head. 'And until they do, the theatre won't ever be the same. I wish Pawel would just tell them where he put it.'

Piotr froze.

Flora touched him gently on the arm.

'You think Pawel Domek took it?' she asked.

Nita shrugged. 'I went out to call my mum for two minutes. You can't make calls on the stage, it's not allowed, so I went out to the stage door lobby. There was no one there. I made my call and went back inside. I didn't see Pawel the whole time, but Wendy saw him on the stairs.' Nita sighed gently. 'I'd understand if it was him. He cares so much about his family back home. I get that. When you want to help people you love, you can do stupid things. But I wish he hadn't.'

Nita pushed herself up out of the chair. She wasn't much taller than Flora, and a good inch or two shorter than Piotr. 'I'd better get back. I'm hiding here, really. But the show must go on. I hope.'

She gave a quick nod in the direction of the counter and then walked out of the shop, her head bent.

Piotr watched Nita leave. She thought Dad did it. But she had to be wrong. She *had* to be.

But if she was telling the truth, why wasn't Dad at the stage door?

Where had he been when the necklace was taken? Was that what Dad was keeping from him?

In his mind, he saw Flora's list of suspects again. With Dad's name at the bottom in teeny, tiny writing. It didn't need to be bigger, did it?

Chapter Fourteen

Andrew didn't have long to wait before Albie Sandbaum left the theatre. He came out of the stage door only moments after Nita.

Andrew whipped open his notebook. *Suspect,* he wrote. *Tall man. Orangey skin. Dark quiff. Nice mac – designer??*

Andrew got up off the bench.

Hungry? Soz roll? No. Passes bakery. Passes gallery, stops to look at tall gallery owner. Carries on walking. Goes into – Fire Station Bar and Grill.

Hmm.

Could a reporter bother a celebrity assistant over a posh meal?

Maybe.

Andrew strolled towards the restaurant. He paused by the big glass window and pretended to retie his shoelace.

The fact his shoes were done up with Velcro didn't bother him at all. He just needed to see what Albie was doing.

Suspect NOT at table. Reading Costume Designer *magazine at bar. Waiter arriving – with brown paper bag. TAKEAWAY – yes!*

Andrew could have done a dance of joy – Albie wasn't staying inside the posh restaurant! But drawing attention to himself by dancing was the exact opposite of what he should be doing. He struggled for a minute. Then he did a little dance of joy anyway.

'Smooth moves,' an American voice said. Albie stood in the doorway, watching Andrew's dance with a wry grin. 'You should be on the stage.'

'Do you really think so?' Andrew asked in amazement.

'No,' Albie said. 'I don't.'

Andrew, ignoring the fact that reporters should do interviews calmly, got annoyed. 'What do you know about it? Who died and made you king of auditions?'

Albie chuckled to himself. It wasn't an entirely happy sound. 'Oh, I've been in enough auditions to write the book on it.'

'Watching Betty Massino?'

'You know I work for her? Well, listen, she doesn't audition. People beg her to be in their shows. No, I've been the auditionee, sweetheart. I've been on the receiving end of *Don't call us, we'll call you* a hundred times.'

Albie was an actor. Or at least he wanted to be an actor.

'Is Betty helping you?'

Albie held up the brown paper bag. Andrew was surprised to notice that Albie had dark flecks under his fingernails – he seemed too fashion-conscious to have mucky nails. 'Not so far,' Albie said. 'You see, I'm a glorified errand boy, fetching lunch. This job is not the hot ticket I thought it would be. I mean, look at me, standing in the freezing cold talking to you.' He gave a visible shudder.

Andrew looked up at the clear blue sky, with its wisps of cotton-wool clouds. 'But it's a nice day!' he objected.

'Not when you're used to Los Angeles,' Albie said. 'This is positively arctic.'

Andrew remembered something with a rush of excitement. 'Is that why you went to fetch a shawl for Betty? On the day her necklace was stolen?'

Albie's face changed in an instant. The wry, cynical grin turned into something much crueller. 'Why are you asking me? Are British cops so badly funded they need to employ kids now?'

Andrew didn't know what to say. 'I'm training to be a reporter, for the local paper. I was hoping I could interview you. I wanted to ask you a few questions.'

'Well, don't. Or I'll have you arrested for harassment.'

'What? Are you serious? I can't get arrested for asking a question!'

Albie wrinkled his nose. 'Can't you? Are you sure?'

Andrew was not sure.

'Well, it's been a joy. Not. I'd better get this steak – well done, with horseradish and pickles on rye – back to Betty before she notices she's hungry. That's what my life has become, you see. When really I should be playing Hamlet.'

Without another word, Albie turned his back on Andrew and stalked back to the stage door, obviously brooding on his fate with every step.

Andrew watched him go. Had he learned anything useful? He looked at the notes he'd been planning on giving to Flora: *black nails, steak on rye, Hamlet, harassment.*

He was pretty sure that nothing good had come of that interview at all.

Chapter Fifteen

'B ... B ... B ...' Minnie said for a while.

She and Sylvie were in the corridor outside wardrobe and Minnie was stuttering at an international star.

It was almost enough to make Minnie forget the photo she'd just seen.

Then Sylvie leaped to her rescue. 'Ms Massino, this is my friend, Minnie. Minnie, this is Ms Betty Massino,' Sylvie added helpfully.

'How wonderful,' Betty Massino said, holding out her hand.

It was a delicate hand with the softest skin that Minnie had ever touched. It made Kasia's baby skin seem like sandpaper. As they shook hands, Minnie felt a weird rush, like stepping off the waltzers. She was actually, genuinely, really, truly shaking hands with a total Hollywood legend. Andrew was going to freak!

'How do you do?' she finally managed to wheeze out.

'Well, to be frank, I've had better days. I remember one vacation, as a girl, we went to a swamp. An alligator ate my popsicle. That was a better day than this one.' There was a slight frown at the edge of Betty's mouth.

'Is it because of your necklace?' Minnie asked. 'I'm sorry you lost it. I mean, you didn't lose it. I mean, I'm sorry it's gone.'

'You're sorry it was stolen? You and me both, sugar. Anyway, it isn't that right now. I just flunked my lines in a read-through like I was a freshman on my first day.' Betty made a noise that was halfway between a hiss and a spit.

Minnie felt her face flush. 'Sorry,' she mumbled again.

Betty flashed a sudden lightbulb smile. 'Oh, honey, don't apologise. I was the one who forgot the lines! Is Sylvie giving you the grand tour?'

Sylvie smiled brightly. 'Minnie's interested in the theatre.'

'Oh,' Betty said. 'Fantastic! Young people today are obsessed with celebrity shows and such. It's grand to meet a fellow theatre-lover. Are you more Brecht or Chekhov?'

Minnie felt as though her throat was getting tighter.

The blush of moments earlier was deepening to full flame-face. How was this going so badly?

'Minnie likes them both,' Sylvie said with a dainty grin.

Betty laughed. It sounded amused, but also kind, as though she'd be ready to take her turn as the butt of a joke. 'Why don't you girls come and have a cup of coffee with me?' she asked. 'Or, this being the UK, I can try to make tea. Probably.' She led the way towards her dressing room and unlocked the door. 'Albie was here somewhere. I don't know where he's got to. But I expect I can make tea without him.'

She filled a kettle at the little sink and switched it on. In a low cupboard with a chipped door, she found some mugs and a teapot. 'I just put the bags in here, right? How many, do you think? Four? Five?'

Sylvie took the teapot from her. 'I can do it,' she said.

Betty settled into the narrow chair in relief. 'I have to say, honey, I'm not too domesticated. My daddy always said I could barbecue water. He wondered why I couldn't cook as well as my mom.'

'That's a bit sexist,' Sylvie said primly.

Betty seemed to almost choke on her laughter. 'I guess it was. Well said, honey.'

Minnie sat on a cushion on the floor, while Sylvie made tea for them all. It was crowded in the little dressing room, but somehow Betty made it feel more like an adventure than a squish.

Betty Massino leaned down, so that her bright brown eyes were level with Minnie's. 'So, tell me,' Betty whispered, 'why are you pretending to like the theatre?'

'She does like it!' Sylvie said quickly.

'Nonsense. Did you see her face when I asked her to choose which playwright she liked best? She looked like I'd asked her to choose her favourite roadkill. Which means she was fibbing. Which also means there's an interesting story here. And I want to hear it.'

Betty took the mug of tea from Sylvie and cupped it with both hands. Her pale, pearl nails somehow managed to look expensive against the stained white crockery.

The actress's smile as she looked at Minnie was warm and real.

'Well,' Minnie began slowly, 'it's all to do with your necklace and Piotr's dad.'

Betty listened as Minnie described the events of the last few days. Every now and then, Minnie wondered if she should be sharing so much – Betty wasn't definitely, absolutely not a suspect, after all. But the actress nodded keenly and gasped in all the right places, so that Minnie couldn't help but trust her.

Soon, the tea was gone and the story was told.

Betty shook her head. 'Poor Piotr. And my poor necklace. *Poof!* Gone. I wonder if I'll ever see it again.'

'Why did you leave it in here on its own?' Sylvie asked.

Betty sighed and sipped her tea. 'I've asked myself that a thousand times. I think it's because a theatre feels like family. You trust people. I had no idea that anyone would take it. And the door was locked, of course.'

'Yes,' Sylvie agreed. 'And Mr Domek was guarding the keys in the lobby. And anyway, how would anyone know the necklace was here?'

Betty's cheeks took on a pinker glow. Minnie was surprised to realise that even famous actresses could blush. 'Well,' she said sadly, 'that was my own fault too. I was such a klutz. I'd booked a cab to take me to the bank. I told people I had something valuable to take there.'

Minnie felt a prickle of something uncomfortable. They'd been in the lobby when Betty ordered the taxi. Had anyone else been there?

'So,' Betty said, 'you're going to clear your friend's dad's name and return my necklace?'

'We hope so. You won't tell anyone, will you?' Minnie said.

'Sure, I won't. This calls for a reward!' Betty said, clapping her hands together.

'But we haven't found it yet,' Sylvie pointed out.

'A down payment, then. Here ...' Betty reached for a few make-up bags and a vanity case. 'I get sent make-up and perfume and hair stuff all the time. Sometimes two or three of the same thing! People want me to say how great their products are, even if they go on like spackle and smell like the floor of a public bus. I keep some of the good stuff, though. You want some?'

Minnie didn't have the heart to tell Betty that Mum had banned her from wearing any make-up until she was sixteen. This was a present from Betty Massino, after all.

Betty pulled out eyeshadows and perfume bottles, lipsticks and nail polishes in all the colours of the rainbow, from peach pale to plum black. 'Take one,' she said.

Minnie reached for a gold-coloured tube that held a pillar-box red lipstick. Sylvie took a set of eyeshadows in shades of brown and beige.

'Thank you,' Minnie said, shy now that the story was told.

'Sure, honey, it's me that should be thanking you. You kids are on my side at least. You know the police turned this whole theatre upside down. Even got a sniffer dog to come and search for my scent on the necklace. But they found nothing. It just vanished into thin air. Can you believe it?'

Just then, the door to the dressing room opened. Albie stood there, key in hand, his hair immaculately quiffed, his mac open to reveal a sharp suit. He was holding a brown paper bag.

'Lunch?' he asked, holding up the bag.

'Oh, Albie, sweetheart, I was just thinking I'm hungry enough to eat a cow mooing in a bun. Aren't you an angel?'

'More kids?' he said, looking at the girls in disgust.

'Sylvie and her young friend are just visiting. Ain't that right?'

Minnie and Sylvie nodded in tandem.

'Well,' Albie said, 'visiting time is over.'

Chapter Sixteen

Piotr wanted to ask Dad about Nita finding the lobby empty on the night of the theft. But he couldn't. Dad was out again. Mum said he was visiting all the Polish people they knew to ask about work back home. Did anyone know of something? Mum made Piotr pack a huge suitcase to take at the weekend. It was too much stuff for a short visit. Were they really going to leave him with his cousins while they packed up the flat here? Mum had said, 'We'll see,' and, 'Please do as you're told.'

So Piotr had done as he was told.

But inside, he burned with questions. Was Nita telling the truth? Had Dad left the stage door lobby? Why?

He had gone to bed without any answers.

Piotr had arranged to meet the others the next morning to share what they'd learned during the interviews.

Andrew, Flora and Sylvie sat in their regular window booth at the cafe. Flora's notebook was open and she was copying Andrew's notes on his interview with Albie. Piotr was ordering drinks at the counter. Minnie was yet to arrive.

'So,' Flora asked, 'was Albie jewel-thief-level rude? Or just out-of-work-actor-level rude?'

Andrew gave a shrug. 'It's difficult to tell. I'm sorry, I didn't find out anything about the theft.'

'Don't worry, you tried.'

Piotr handed out the drinks. The cafe door opened, the bell above it tinkled and Minnie waltzed into the room.

'We had tea with Betty,' Minnie said with a smile wide enough to bridge a river.

'*Betty Massino?!*' Andrew gasped.

'No, Betty from the fish stall. *Of course* Betty Massino.' Minnie practically pirouetted into a seat. 'She gave us presents! She let us choose from her make-up bag. Lipsticks, eyeshadows, nail varnish, anything!'

'Sylvie!' Andrew said. 'Why didn't you tell us?'

Sylvie smirked. 'Oh, I've often had tea with Betty. It just didn't occur to me to say.'

'Huh?' Minnie sounded outraged.

Flora glanced desperately between Sylvie and Minnie. Then she picked up her pen and asked quickly, 'What did she tell you about the theft?'

Minnie's glare lifted a little. 'Well, she didn't know much. But she told us how sad she was about it being stolen.'

'Well, that's hardly breaking news,' Andrew said with disdain.

'You're just jealous because I drank tea, and got a lipstick.'

'A lipstick?' Andrew said crossly. 'You were supposed to be interviewing Wendy. You were supposed to be rescuing Piotr from being Gdansked.'

Minnie's grin became a frown. How dare Andrew suggest that she didn't care about Piotr! 'Well, I did that too! I found a real clue!'

'What? Where?' Flora said.

'In wardrobe. There was a photo behind Wendy's desk. Oh, I took a whole load of photos on my phone: Wendy's desk and some of the weird things in wardrobe – nail varnish, a proper deerstalker hat. I'll send them to your phone, Flora.'

'Great. I'll put them in the notebook.'

'What was Wendy's photo of?' Piotr asked.

Minnie spread her hands dramatically. 'It was a photo of Wendy, with her arm around a man. And I know who the man was. It was Big Phil!'

'Who's Big Phil?' Sylvie asked.

Now Minnie looked at Sylvie in pity. Even Piotr gave a small shake of his head.

Andrew spoke. 'You don't know Big Phil? Everyone knows him! He's a trader.'

'Mum says he's nothing but a gangster,' Minnie said. 'He'll tell you he's got a good offer on conditioning shampoo or the softest cotton towels imported straight from Egypt, and then, when it turns up, it's basically washing-up liquid and some tea towels.'

'Why does your mum order from him, then?' Sylvie asked.

Minnie pressed her lips together tightly.

Andrew answered. 'Because, if you don't use him as a supplier, then you can't be sure your shop will stay in one piece.'

'A protection racket?' Sylvie said, her mouth hanging open.

'What's a protection racket?' Flora asked, her pen scribbling furiously.

'It was in a play we did once. It means you pay gangsters

to help look after your business, and if you don't pay they make sure your business fails.'

'And Wendy had her arm around this man?' Flora asked.

Minnie nodded. 'It was Big Phil all right. And she was smiling like anything.'

Piotr had been twisting the corners of a paper napkin while he listened to Minnie. Now, he felt a shiver of excitement and pushed the napkin aside. 'Nita said something about someone at the theatre having a brother who was trouble. What was it, Flora?'

Flora flicked through her notebook. 'She said she was having a row with someone who had enough on her plate with their brother.'

'Wendy said she'd been rowing with Nita,' Sylvie said. 'Do you think Big Phil might be her brother?'

'Wendy was the one who accused Piotr's dad too!' Minnie said. 'She said she'd seen him in the corridor outside the company dressing rooms when he had no business being there.'

'If she'd stolen the necklace, it would make sense to throw the blame on someone else!' Andrew added.

Piotr felt a surge of hope. Wendy might have been lying when she said she'd seen Dad! She might be Suspect Number One!

'So, this Big Philip,' Sylvie said.

'Big Phil,' Minnie corrected witheringly.

'Phil, Philip, whatever.' Sylvie waved a hand. 'He's a proper gangster?'

'What did you say?' Piotr asked.

Sylvie frowned. 'A proper gangster?'

'No, before that.'

'Whatever.'

'Before that.'

'Big Philip.'

Piotr wriggled. He put his hand in his back pocket. Then paused. He hadn't told anyone about the card. The one he'd been carrying around for a few days now, next to Jimmy Wright's. The one he had accidentally taken from Betty's dressing room. The one signed by Philip.

He was going to have to tell them.

Would they be shocked? Would they think, *Like father, like son*? That neither of them could be trusted? That they were both thieves?

What if they didn't want to help him after that? What if they decided it'd be better if he did go to Poland – and good riddance?

Was accidentally stealing just as bad as deliberately stealing?

He reached into his back pocket and took out the good-luck card.

It was looking scuffed at the edges, and the whole thing was bent where he'd been sitting on it. He laid it on the table and tried to smooth it flat.

'What's that?' Sylvie asked.

There were veiny creases right across the picture of the woman and her necklace. He hadn't just taken it, he'd ruined it.

'I didn't mean to,' Piotr said. His stomach felt knotted and tight. 'I was holding it when Albie found us in the dressing room. I just ran. I'm sorry.'

The words came out in a rush.

Sylvie plucked the card from his hands and opened it.

'What's it say?' Andrew asked.

Piotr looked at his friends. They didn't even seem to notice what he'd said. 'I took it,' he tried again.

'Yes,' Andrew said. 'But what does it say inside?'

Oh.

Piotr waited.

'"Looking forward to watching you 'Sparkle'. Your biggest fan, Philip",' Sylvie read. She seemed not to be the slightest bit bothered that he'd stolen it.

His friends were brilliant. Even Sylvie.

'Philip? Big Phil?' Flora suggested. 'It's a bit creepy. Like stalking, or something,' Flora said thoughtfully. 'Do you think he was trying to run a protection racket at the theatre? Saying to Betty that he'd guard her necklace if she paid him?'

Andrew slammed his palm down on the table. 'But she didn't pay! And the necklace was stolen.'

'But how would Big Phil get in? Without anyone seeing him?' Flora asked.

'Wendy,' Minnie said with certainty.

'So,' Flora said, looking at her notebook, 'how do we prove it? How do we show that Wendy helped the real thief?'

There was no reply straight away. Piotr was twisting his napkin again. The others drank slowly, or looked at the steam and smoke rising over the counter. Every now and again, Ellie, the owner, shouted an order number across the cafe and someone got up to fetch their fry-up or their toasted teacake. But their table was deep in thought.

'A confession,' Andrew said, at last. 'We need to get her to confess.'

'Why would she do that?' Minnie said. 'As far as she knows, she's got away with it.'

Minnie was right, Piotr thought. Wendy wouldn't just

stroll into a police station and admit to stealing Betty's jewels. It was never going to happen. They would have to be smart to catch these thieves.

'We need hard evidence, then,' Andrew said. 'We need to find the jewels in her handbag.'

Minnie rolled her eyes. 'Yes, I'm sure she has them in her purse, next to her bus pass and breath mints. The police searched everyone, remember? The jewels are hidden, or were thrown out of a window to an accomplice before anyone noticed they'd been stolen.'

'Fair point,' Andrew admitted.

Piotr thought about Big Phil again. Did he have the jewels? Or were they still with Wendy?

'We're going to need to pay a visit to Big Phil,' Piotr said finally.

They all turned to look at him, Andrew and Sylvie's eyes wide, Minnie's mouth open, Flora's pale skin turning even paler.

'What?' Minnie said finally.

She appeared to be speaking for everyone.

'We need to pay a visit to Big Phil and find out whether Wendy did pass on the jewels to him. If we can spot him with them, well, then ...' Piotr trailed off into silence.

'I can see you've thought this through,' Minnie said.

'We don't challenge him, or anything. If we see anything suspicious, then we can go to the police and report it to them.'

Andrew shook his head and leaned back against the seat. 'The police aren't going to listen to us. They'll think we're just kids interfering in other people's business. They'll just tell us off for being nosey and our parents will ground us.'

Piotr thought of Jimmy Wright, the police officer who had visited their flat to interview Dad. He'd been kind; he'd smiled sympathetically. And, more importantly, he'd said that if anything occurred to Piotr about the crime, he should call Jimmy. He pulled Jimmy's card from his pocket and put it on the table.

'The police will listen,' Piotr said firmly. 'We need to watch Big Phil and see what he does, where he goes.'

'Who's going to go? I can't,' Andrew said forlornly. 'My mum needs me back now for physio.'

'I've got rehearsals,' Sylvie said. 'And Flora has a piano lesson.'

'Of course she does,' Minnie said, rolling her eyes.

Flora slipped the good-luck card and Jimmy's card inside her notebook.

'I guess it's me and you then, Minnie,' Piotr said. 'Any ideas where to start?'

'Last time we had a delivery of washing-up liquid pretending to be hair relaxer, Dad said he'd go to Big Phil's lock-up to complain. Mum told him not to be so silly and we used the stuff to clean plates for months.'

'What's a lock-up?' Piotr asked.

Minnie pulled out her phone. 'Let's find out,' she said.

Chapter Seventeen

In seconds, Minnie had found a definition. 'Well,' she said, after flicking through entries, '*Lock-Up* is the name of a rubbish-looking film. Lock up can also mean going to prison. And, hey, I think this might be it: it means a garage or railway arch used for storage.'

'There are five or six arches where the railway climbs up towards the station,' Andrew said. 'It's only a few streets away, behind the market.'

Minnie grinned. 'I know where you mean – they've got big wooden doors, painted green. That would be the perfect place to store stolen jewellery.'

'As long as he hasn't sold it already,' Piotr said grimly.

Minnie leaped up and tucked her phone into her back pocket. 'There's only one way to find out,' she said. 'Let's go. Flora, I'll send you more pictures for the notebook. And text you anything suspicious.'

Piotr and Minnie left the others and headed out of the cafe.

Two streets beyond the market, the railway tracks cut through the town. Neat, brick bridges lifted the tracks, letting traffic pass below. Wires ran high above, like tightropes. Instead of following the road up towards the station, Piotr and Minnie took a footpath that headed down. Towards the arches. The tarmac was scruffy and crumbling as though the grass were nibbling its edges.

'Dad's booked plane tickets for Saturday,' Piotr said quietly. As they walked, he kept his eyes straight ahead, not looking at Minnie. 'We're going in two days.'

'No, you aren't,' Minnie said firmly. 'We'll save you.'

He wished he could believe her.

The path turned and they saw the arches – high sweeps of brickwork, the cavernous mouths shut in by huge wooden doors. There were five arches in all. In front of them was a small car park, or a turning circle, or a dead end, depending on how you looked at it. A narrow road led away from the car park.

There was no one about.

'Which do you think is Big Phil's?' Minnie whispered.

Piotr looked at the five doors. Most looked unloved:

peeling paint and chipped woodwork, padlocks that had rusted to marmalade-orange.

But there was one that seemed better kept.

He walked over to it. The green paint was glossy and smooth. The plate-lock sparkled and the padlock looked brand new. It was definitely in use.

He lifted the padlock.

The metal plate it was attached to swung out towards him.

The door wasn't locked!

Then he heard the voice.

Piotr froze, the hard metal of the padlock felt like ice in his hand. He let go, ever so gently.

It was a deep, gravelly, male voice coming from inside the lock-up. 'We said Thursday,' the man was saying. 'And today is Thursday. We have an appointment.'

Piotr wondered who he was talking to. There was no reply. It must be a phone call. Unless the person *couldn't* talk. They might be tied to a chair with their hands roped behind them and a gag in their mouth. Piotr felt a strange tingling in his legs. Like water where his knees should be. He wondered if they were about to collapse under him. He forced himself to stand steady and listen.

'No,' the man said, 'we were clear as crystal. The goods need to be shifted.'

Minnie joined Piotr by the door and they searched for a chink in the wood. For a moment it appeared to have no holes, but then Minnie saw a slight gap. She positioned her eye close to the door hinge. As Piotr moved closer to her, she stepped aside to let him see.

Inside was dark, lit only by a desk lamp angled away from them. In the gloom, he could make out the hulking shape of a man mountain.

Big Phil.

His huge body made it impossible to see anything else. He might have had a whole array of stolen jewels, a goldsmith's counter racked with gems in there with him, but the leather jacket and swollen neck filled Piotr's line of sight.

Big Phil's shaved head was pressed against a mobile phone that looked like a toy in the hulking fist.

'The Sparkles will make my fortune, but the police have been sniffing around Wendy.'

Piotr suppressed a gasp.

Sparkles! Did he mean the necklace?

Was this enough to go to Jimmy with?

No.

One overheard phone call was hardly a confession. What they needed was to get inside and find the stolen goods.

Could they do that now?

Piotr moved away, waving silently at Minnie to follow. There was a dusty, rambling buddleia growing on a bit of wasteland by the road. Its dripping purple flowers were a perfect curtain to hide behind.

Piotr lifted a branch and crept into the green gloom of the bush. There were a few limp crisp packets on the ground and an empty plastic bottle, and just enough room for a whispered conversation.

'Did you hear him? He said he's got the necklace!' Piotr said.

Minnie frowned a little, her mouth pulled to one side. 'He didn't say that exactly.'

'What else would "Sparkles" be?'

'Fireworks?'

'Fireworks won't make his fortune! He said he was worried about the police talking to Wendy. That can't be to do with fireworks.'

Minnie nodded, a little reluctantly, Piotr thought. But he was so certain he was right. He just had to be! 'We need to investigate the lock-up.'

'How would we get in – with Big Phil sat there?'

Piotr grinned.

He had an idea.

He slunk back out of the buddleia.

He looked at the road, at the footpath, to check the coast was clear.

Then he raced over to the green door, silently slipped the padlock off the lock, gripped it in his fist and raced back to their hiding place. His heart was thumping hard as he crouched next to Minnie again.

He opened his fist, where the padlock gleamed like stolen treasure.

'Now he can't lock the lock-up. He'll come out, see the padlock is missing, and he'll need to go to a shop, or something, to get a new one. While he's doing that, we can go inside.'

'Risky,' Minnie said. 'I like it.'

Piotr's legs had started to go to sleep before Big Phil came out. He twisted and bent a few times to get rid of the pins and needles.

'Shh,' Minnie hissed. 'Here he comes.'

Big Phil grunted in annoyance as he realised his padlock was missing. He lurched around, looking for it on the ground. He swore loudly. He pushed the door closed.

Then he marched off towards the market without a backwards glance.

'Now,' Piotr said.

They crept out of the foliage and edged towards the lock-up.

Minnie pulled the huge door open, just a crack, and the two of them slipped inside.

The door was the only source of light, so they kept it open a tiny bit. They couldn't risk turning on the desk lamp.

'We've only got about five minutes,' Minnie said. 'There's a hardware stall at the market. Big Phil could be back pretty soon with a padlock. We could get trapped in here if we're not careful.'

The idea of being shut in the dark, in a gangster's lock-up, was enough to make the hairs on the back of Piotr's neck bristle with fear.

'Fine,' he said, with a heavy swallow. 'Let's look for the necklace.'

The lock-up was part storeroom, part workshop. On one wall was a bank of plastic boxes, each neatly labelled with wipe-clean marker. Piotr recognised the handwriting from the card – Big Phil was definitely 'Phillip'. Minnie hurriedly took snapshots with her phone. Piotr could read the labels in the camera's flash: *soap – shampoo, carpet cleaner, nit treatment; chalk – indigestion, blackboard, pub signs; rocks – crystal healing, paperweights, lucky charms.*

On another wall was a selection of power tools. Each tool had its place marked out with a thick, black line, like the body outline of a murder victim. Piotr hoped the drill was just used for hanging pictures.

In the centre of the room, taking up most of the space, was a meticulously built tower of a dozen or so cardboard boxes. Piotr lifted the flap of the top box. Inside were empty plastic bottles, without labels.

They must be for whatever the next knock-off, bogus product was that he would try to sell.

To one side stood a big desk, where Big Phil had been sitting while they spied on him. On it lay a row of pencils, each set at a sharp right angle to the edge of the wood. A clean margarine tub full of metal ball bearings was placed neatly beside them. Minnie stepped closer and, though her hand hovered over the pencils, she didn't touch any of them. 'Piotr,' she whispered, 'the points on the pencils are all exactly the same length.' Her voice sounded a little awed. Piotr, who had seen the mess inside her pencil case, wasn't surprised.

'Big Phil has got to be the neatest gangster in the world,' Piotr said finally.

There wasn't a speck of dirt on the concrete floor, or a tool, box or pencil out of place. It had the precision of an operating theatre.

There was no way they could move a single thing without Big Phil knowing someone had been there.

'We have to look, though,' Minnie said. 'We can't take this risk and go home with nothing.'

'It's the *getting home* part that I'm worried about,' Piotr said.

But she was right. 'Let's try the desk drawers first.'

Piotr gripped a metal handle and pulled the drawer out. It moved soundlessly, as though it had been oiled. Which it probably had been, Piotr supposed.

Inside the drawer were neat stacks of paper, their edges perfectly aligned. The paper on top was from an internet firm confirming delivery of a sack of flour. He didn't dare lift that sheet as it lay perfectly square, like a block of printer paper, on top of those below.

He slid the drawer closed and opened the next one.

Stationery. As carefully arranged as a town plan.

Below that – a plastic box!

Exactly the sort of thing you might keep a stolen necklace in! Buttybox-sized, with flipped-down tabs to hold it closed.

Piotr flipped up the flip-down tabs and lifted the lid with a pounding heart.

Sandwiches.

Cheese and pickle. Wrapped in clingfilm.

Piotr could barely speak with frustration. The proof to clear Dad's name had to be in here – it just had to be and he couldn't stomach the idea of going home without it.

'Hey, Piotr,' Minnie whispered.

She was at the other end of the long desk. She was holding up a *Slimmers' World* magazine with a picture of a smiley, skinny model on the front. 'Looks like Big Phil wants to be Little Phil,' she said.

'What's that underneath?' Piotr moved closer. There was a black book under the magazine. He opened it. A diary. Each page was for a day of the week, with the hours down the side. Tiny, all-caps handwriting had filled in appointments. Today's entries read: *DENTIST 2 P.M.; WILD-DOG MURPHY 6.30 P.M.; MAD ANDY 8 P.M.*

'This is a record of where he's been! And who he's been seeing!' Minnie said, hardly able to control a squeal.

'Look at Monday, the day of the robbery,' Piotr insisted.

They turned the page quickly. There was only one entry on Monday. *RETURN LIBRARY BOOKS.*

Oh.

Maybe it was a code? Piotr thought hopefully.

Or maybe he hadn't met up with Wendy yet? Piotr remembered the phone call they'd overheard. Perhaps Big Phil was worried about the police sniffing around Wendy because *she* still had the necklace?

His eyes scanned back through the diary entries, but there was nothing that could refer to a meeting with Wendy – not unless she used a nickname like 'Angry Dave' or 'Razor Bill'.

It didn't seem likely.

Then, flicking forward through the week, his eyes fell on four words.

OPENING NIGHT. MEET W.

The entry was for Friday – tomorrow.

The night the play started.

Minnie and Piotr's eyes met with a flash of excitement. It looked like Wendy still had the necklace and would be giving it to Big Phil on opening night.

They gave each other a soft, silent high-five.

And that was when they heard the sound of whistling. The sort of whistling done by a huge man in a leather jacket returning with a new padlock.

Chapter Eighteen

'He's back!' Piotr whispered.

The door was ajar.

They stopped just inside and listened.

The whistling was close. On the footpath.

The footpath that had an excellent view of the lock-ups.

If they ran for it, Big Phil would see them. And chase them.

And catch them.

And then who knew what? He'd be furious. They may even find themselves in sacks at the bottom of the canal.

Piotr looked around wildly.

There was no other exit.

They were trapped.

'Wait here,' Minnie said.

Where else was he going to go?

She turned back to the desk and picked up the tub of ball bearings. They were perfect, metallic spheres, like silver marbles. 'When I say "run", we run. And along the road, not the path. OK?'

Away from Big Phil.

It made sense.

Although he wasn't sure how the ball bearings came into it.

Minnie held up the tub. She peered around the open door, out towards the path, and the whistling man.

She took one ball bearing and hurled it towards a tree beside the path. It hit it with a sharp thunk. The branches of the tree rustled as though a squirrel had had a sudden shock.

'Eh?' Big Phil said, turning away from the lock-ups to look at the tree.

Minnie threw another. This time it bounced off the bark and landed in the undergrowth.

Big Phil bent to look.

Minnie sent the whole box flying hard in the air. A shower of metal shot rained down on Big Phil. He cowered under his leather jacket, shrieking like a car alarm as the metal pinged off him.

'Run!' Minnie barked.

Piotr needed no more instruction. They both pelted away from the lock-up on to the gravel road.

Big Phil peeked out from under his protective jacket.

'Hey!' he yelled. 'Hey!'

He set off after them.

And stepped right on to the splatter of ball bearings.

His feet flew out from under him.

He landed – *thump* – on his back.

Piotr could hear the wheezy coughs of the winded gangster as he and Minnie raced away.

The road curled left and, within a hundred paces, opened on to the high street.

They were soon lost in the fabric, colour and movement of the street.

Minnie glanced back once or twice. There was no sign of Big Phil. She put out a hand and they slowed to a walk. Their breath was raggedy from the running and, for a while, neither of them spoke.

Then Minnie said, 'Do you think he saw us?'

'Yes.'

'But do you think he saw us enough to recognise us, I mean? Does he know who we are?'

Piotr felt cold, despite the running.

'We need to be on the lookout for him,' Piotr said

finally. 'Even if he did see us, we didn't take anything, or break anything in his lock-up. With any luck, he'll think we were just mucking about. Silly kids. That's all. He won't know we're on to him.'

'Are we? On to him, I mean?' Minnie asked. 'Do you think the diary was real evidence?'

Piotr thought about the plane tickets Dad had printed out and stuck to the fridge. He thought about the suitcase on his bed. The room being prepared at his cousins' house. 'It's evidence,' Piotr said grimly. 'He's meeting Wendy tomorrow night. He's going to the show. She must be planning on giving him the necklace then. All we have to do is catch them red-handed and then everyone will know that Dad is innocent.'

'Then we need to get some tickets for the theatre!' Minnie said.

Chapter Nineteen

Piotr was awake early. The sun was up, but there was still a long while to go before he could call it breakfast time. He got up anyway. He was too testy to sleep. He pulled on the jeans and T-shirt that Mum had left unpacked. His last full day.

He wouldn't think about that now.

He had to believe they'd find the necklace tonight. The alternative was too horrible.

He let himself out of the flat and walked downstairs. It was too early to see any of the neighbours. Most would still be in pyjamas, dreaming of knights and dragons.

It was good to be alone. Like the whole town was there just for him.

He pulled his jacket closer. The sun wasn't high enough yet to be hot and he had goosebumps in the shadows. At the play park, he sat down on a swing and watched the thick, white clouds scud across the sky. At least the sky was the same in Poland. He set the swing moving, with his legs stretched out straight.

'No friends today?'

He let the swing slow.

Jimmy Wright was unlocking his car. 'On your own?'

Piotr nodded.

'How are you getting on?'

He shrugged in reply.

'Well, it's been good to chat,' Jimmy said with a grin.

He opened his car door and was about to climb inside when Piotr shouted, 'Wait!'

Piotr stopped the swing, using his foot as a skidding brake.

Jimmy waited, with one leg in the car and the other on the tarmac. 'What is it, Piotr?'

'Have you found the necklace yet? Have you found the thief?'

Jimmy didn't answer.

'You don't still think Dad did it?'

Still no answer.

'He didn't!' Piotr said. 'He didn't do it!'

Jimmy gave a small smile. 'The thing is, your dad, he isn't very forthcoming. He said he was at his desk, but later admitted he wasn't.'

Dad had told Jimmy he wasn't by the stage door? Nita was right then! Piotr gripped the swing's chains. They felt cold against his skin.

'I'm sorry,' Jimmy said.

'That doesn't mean he was stealing the necklace.'

'I know. And we haven't found his fingerprints at the scene of the crime, just Betty's and Albie's, as you'd expect. We haven't any hard evidence against your dad. That's why we haven't arrested him yet ... See you later, Piotr,' Jimmy said and got into his car.

Yet. Jimmy had said *yet*.

Chapter Twenty

It turned out that the show was already a total and complete sell-out. There wasn't a single, solitary seat left for sale. They wouldn't get in even if they stood at the back or sat on each other's laps.

Piotr and Andrew walked away from the theatre. The girl behind the counter had almost managed to hide her grin when they'd asked for tickets for the opening night of a play starring Betty Massino. Almost. But she obviously thought it was hilarious.

'It sold out about six months ago, I'm sorry,' the girl said. 'It *is* Betty Massino, you know.'

They knew.

They knew well enough.

So, tonight Big Phil would meet up with Wendy, take the necklace from her and disappear off into gangland with it, never to be seen again. And tomorrow morning, Piotr would be boarding a flight to Poland.

'It's not fair!' he said, kicking a stray stone on the pavement.

'We're not done yet,' Andrew said. 'There are more ways than one to skin a cat.'

'Why would anyone want to skin a cat?'

'I have no clue.'

They walked as far as the salon. They could see Minnie inside, rearranging nail varnishes at the nail bar. Her mum was busy clipping at someone's hair. They pushed open the door.

'Alphabetical order?' Andrew asked, nodding at the bottles in Minnie's hand.

'No. Ugliest first.' She held up a raw-steak-burgundy glitter. 'Did you get the tickets?'

Andrew flopped down into a stylist's chair. It spun gently beneath his weight. 'No. Sold out.'

'Oi,' Minnie's mum said, 'that's not a fairground ride.'

'Sorry,' Andrew said and went to sit in the window seat with Piotr.

Minnie clicked the varnish bottles together, jiggling for space. 'You've spoken to Sylvie and Flora, I suppose?'

Piotr smiled. *Of course.* There was another way to skin the cat – with Sylvie. *If* she agreed to help them, of course.

'Can you call Flora? She's probably the best one to ask for a favour,' he said.

Minnie pulled out her phone and dialled. Soon, she was explaining to Flora what they needed.

At the other end of the line, Flora paused for a moment. Then she said, 'I have a ticket and we've one for our au pair. She might give us her seat – she doesn't get on that well with Sylvie. They're good seats, near the front. Mum was offered tickets, but she's going to watch from the wings, to support Sylvie. I suppose I could ask whether it's too late to get those tickets back. I can't promise, though.'

'I know you can't promise, but thank you for giving it a shot!'

Minnie hung up. 'You know, Sylvie might be the one who gets all the attention, but Flora is pretty amazing. She's going to try to get us in.'

There was a tense wait while they stared at Minnie's phone, willing Flora to call back with good news.

Eventually, the phone rang. Flora. Minnie answered it and listened for a moment. Then her face split into a grin. 'They said yes?' she squealed. 'Flora, you're a star! Thank you, thank you, thank you. Yes, we'll meet you there.' She turned to her mum anxiously. 'I can go, can't I?'

Her mum chuckled. 'I don't know where this sudden interest in plays has come from, but if your friend wants to take you, and you don't show us up, then you can go.'

'A night at the theatre!' Andrew said. 'What should I wear?'

Chapter Twenty-One

Piotr didn't have an answer for Andrew's fashion problem. Since when did he have a clue about clothes? As most of his clothes were packed, he'd be wearing the jeans he'd put on that morning.

They arranged to meet outside the theatre at 7 p.m., then they each went home to get ready.

Piotr let himself into the flat and listened.

He could hear music coming from the living room.

Classical music.

Dad.

Piotr closed the front door slowly. He couldn't hear Kasia's chatter, or Mum moving around. Was Dad home alone?

The sound of low strings throbbed like a bruise. The volume was turned up loud enough for the neighbours to complain. Double basses and cellos calling to the violins.

Beethoven. Dad's favourite.

Piotr walked into the living room. It smelled of bleach cleaner and polish. Every surface was shining, even the windows gleamed. Mum and Dad had been doing a huge tidy. Mum hated coming back to a dirty flat after they'd been away. It depressed her. So she always went over the top on the cleaning before holidays. Not that they were going on holiday. Piotr didn't even know if he'd be coming back.

Dad was sitting in an armchair, music blaring from a phone plugged into a portable speaker. Dad's eyes were closed, his fingers steepled together in front of his chest. He looked as though he were drinking in the music.

A man began singing, joining wind instruments, then the chorus rose above the orchestra. Piotr glanced at the windows, wondering if they were rattling.

Dad spoke without opening his eyes. '*Alle Menschen werden Brüder* – that's what they're singing.' He had to raise his voice over the sound of the chorus.

It wasn't Polish. Piotr didn't know what it meant.

Dad opened his eyes and smiled. He reached over and lowered the volume a little. Insistent horns pulsed on regardless.

'It's German. It means, "All men shall become brothers," Pietrucha. It's a nice thought, don't you think?'

Piotr didn't know what to say. The empty flat seemed to be its own answer.

Dad smiled sadly.

For some reason, Piotr felt a lump form in his own throat. He didn't know what to do with his hands. He sat down heavily on the sofa.

The music ended. Then, after a heartbeat, another piece started, this time more gentle, strings wrapped around each other like treacle around a spoon. A violin played impossibly high notes.

'You're still scared to leave?' Dad asked. It wasn't really a question, though.

Piotr shrugged.

'It won't be how you think it will be. Nothing ever is. But you'll like Poland. You'll go to a good school. You'll make friends. You'll see proper mountains, proper forests. Have a proper life, where no one thinks you're worth less than they are.'

It was the most that Piotr had heard Dad say in a while.

'But, *Tatuś*,' Piotr said, the baby-ish form of 'Dad' surprising him – he hadn't called Dad that for years – 'I have a proper life here. I really do. This *is* home for me, and I don't feel less important than anyone.'

'For now. It will be different as you get older.'

Piotr shook his head. He didn't believe that. 'It might be like that in Poland, though. I won't speak the same as everyone else. I won't know how to do things. Everything will be foreign.'

Dad gave a small start. He drew his fingers across the sandpaper stubble of his chin. 'I suppose it might be. For a while.' He spoke softly.

'And not just for me,' Piotr insisted. 'For you too. You haven't lived there for years. Lots will have changed.' Piotr felt this was his last chance. Dad was actually listening to him.

Dad looked out of the window.

It was a sign that the conversation was over.

Piotr wasn't ready for it to be over. He remembered what Jimmy had said about Dad holding things back. Jimmy was right. Dad was like a jar with the lid screwed on too tight sometimes.

But Piotr had to try.

'Dad, where were you when the necklace was stolen?'

Dad's grey eyes looked shocked. 'What are you asking me?'

'Nita said you weren't at your desk.'

'Does that make you suspicious?' Dad's voice shook slightly.

'No!' Piotr was surprised by how loud his answer was. Almost as loud as a German chorus. The word seemed to jump out of his mouth without him thinking. Of course he wasn't suspicious of Dad. Even with what Nita and Jimmy had said. He'd never really thought Dad was guilty. Piotr felt a weight lift from him. He hadn't believed it deep down. He was glad to realise that. 'No,' he said again, more quietly. 'Wherever you were, I know you had a good reason.'

Dad gave a short laugh. It had absolutely zero humour in it. 'You're a good boy, Pietrucha. I'll tell you where I was. You can decide if it was a good reason to leave my post or not.'

Dad turned off the music.

The sudden silence was shocking.

'I was in the wings,' Dad said. 'I had no right to be there. I shouldn't have been there. But I went anyway, because I wanted to see Betty Massino act. I was as stupidly star-struck as everyone else.'

'Have you told the police?' Piotr was astounded. Dad hadn't been doing anything illegal, anything dangerous; he'd just been watching a rehearsal in a theatre!

'I did. But I was stupid. I let them think I was at my desk. They later found out I wasn't. By then it was too late … It doesn't matter. They're right to blame me. I didn't steal the necklace, but I wasn't doing my job properly,' Dad said sternly.

And, Piotr realised, there was nothing worse for someone like Dad than not doing his job properly.

'But we'll have a new start soon,' Dad said, brightening up. 'Everything will be different at home.'

'Can I see Andrew and Minnie tonight?' Piotr said. 'I'd like to say goodbye.'

Dad smiled. 'Of course. The flight's at two o'clock tomorrow.'

Chapter Twenty-Two

Flora was outside the theatre. She had four tickets in her hand and was clutching them tightly to make sure she didn't lose any. The crowd around her were chattering and laughing as they went to collect tickets, or find friends. Flora stood on tiptoe on the broad stone step, watching anxiously for Piotr, Minnie and Andrew.

'Are you all right?' a voice asked.

A man in a police uniform stood beside her. He had light brown hair and a concerned smile.

'Oh, I'm perfectly all right, thank you,' Flora said, in her best talking-to-an-adult voice. 'I'm just waiting.'

'As long as you're not lost,' the man said. 'There are a few police officers here tonight, what with an international star taking to the stage. But we can make time to help lost children find their parents.'

Flora smiled.

‘I’m Special Constable Jimmy Wright,’ the man said.

‘Oh! Your name is on the card.’

‘What card?’

‘In my notebook!’ Flora was delighted to recognise the name.

‘What notebook?’ Jimmy asked.

Flora felt her face blush pink. Was she supposed to tell the police that they were investigating too? She wasn’t sure the others would be happy with her if she did.

‘Is it a secret?’ Jimmy asked kindly.

Flora nodded.

‘Well, I can’t ask you to share a secret.’

‘Thank you,’ Flora said gratefully.

‘You hold on to those tickets. And enjoy the show. I’m not sure it’s going to be my thing. I prefer action films, myself. But it’s nice to be paid to watch Betty Massino.’

Jimmy gave a quick wave as he skipped up the steps into the grand foyer.

Flora saw Piotr and Andrew walking up Marsh Road. Andrew bounced on the soles of his feet as though he were spring-loaded. He couldn’t stop smiling.

‘I’ve told him we’re here to work,’ Piotr said. ‘But he won’t listen.’

'I will, I will, but we're also going to see Betty Massino make her British stage debut! This is an important moment in entertainment history. And we'll be there! In the good seats!'

'We won't be sitting for long. We'll have to watch Wendy like hawks. Two of us'll need to get backstage. And two will need to find Big Phil and follow him. We won't be watching the stage.'

Minnie arrived next. She'd made a special effort, with a sparkly black top and her best trainers. 'I've never been to the theatre. Only panto at the Community Hall in Year Three and that made me cry,' Minnie said happily. 'I was scared of the shouting. But this – this is going to be amazing.'

Piotr sighed.

None of them had properly realised what failure tonight would mean. This was his last chance to stay in the country. This wasn't a trip to Center Parcs. This wasn't a holiday, or a day at the beach. This was his life they were trying to save.

'Keep an eye out for Wendy or Big Phil,' he said grimly.

All around them were men in suits and ladies in butterfly-coloured dresses. Strings of lights swagged the trees around the theatre, the glow reflected in earrings and brooches, watches and polished shoes. It was as though everyone was touched by a little bit of stage magic.

Flora handed out their tickets. 'There are two good seats, near the front. But because Mum only just asked for the other two, they're rubbish seats. Sorry.'

'Doesn't matter,' Piotr said. 'Andrew can sit in one of those. It will help him focus.'

Flora smiled gratefully. With her red hair pulled into two tight plaits, and a velvet dress, she looked straight out of a Sunday night telly costume drama.

Flora noticed him looking at her clothes. 'Mum made me wear it,' she said, plucking limply at the fabric. 'She gets funny ideas sometimes. Especially when she's stressed. And she's stressed. She's with Sylvie backstage.'

'Is Sylvie stressed?' Andrew asked.

Flora laughed. 'She's having the time of her life! You should see how many flowers everyone's been sent. There's so much foliage you can practically hear parrots back there.'

Piotr read the ticket. The name of the play was written in huge letters across the front, then the date, time and seat number in a smaller font.

Minnie gave a sudden shriek and ducked behind Andrew. 'There he is!' she hissed.

Piotr looked. Big Phil had parked his tiny car in a lay-by and was struggling to get out of the driver's seat. It looked as though the steering wheel was trying to pin him down and he was fighting back.

Piotr turned his back quickly. Minnie was still tucked behind Andrew.

'Do you think he'll recognise us?' Minnie whispered.

'I don't know. But I think it's best if Andrew and Flora stick with Big Phil, and we look for Wendy,' Piotr said.

Minnie was barely visible behind Andrew, but he thought she nodded in agreement; the others agreed too.

'We'll miss the play,' Andrew said a little forlornly.

'Well, if we find Betty Massino's lost necklace, then we'll make the front page of tomorrow's paper,' Piotr pointed out. 'And you'll get to keep me.'

Andrew nodded. A front-page photo of them returning the actress's jewels would be a fair swap for a good view of the play. He cheered up and did a quiet jig across the marble steps. He'd never in a million years have thought he'd be here tonight. He saluted Piotr with three fingers to his forehead.

'Flora and I are on it,' he said. 'Looks like it's me and

you, kid,' he said to Flora, who did look a lot more like a kid than usual, with her centre-parted plaits.

'Hush, here he comes,' she said.

Andrew and Flora stood side by side. They waited on the steps, until Big Phil had struggled his way out of his car, locked it and patted himself down to find his ticket.

Trying their best not to look suspicious, or attract any attention, Andrew and Flora followed him into the foyer. There were plenty of people to pretend to be with. And it was easy to keep the great bulk of Big Phil in view – he was like a shaved bear walking through the foyer.

Carved pillars propped up the elaborate gold plaster ceiling high above the crowd. Big Phil headed towards a curved staircase that ran up the side of the foyer. Andrew and Flora followed. The thick red carpet meant they made no noise, and the swell of chatter from the foyer below disguised their eager whispers.

'He's going to the gods,' Flora said.

'What do you mean?'

'That's what they call the cheap seats – you're so high up that you're next to the gods. Those are where our seats are too.'

An usher stood next to a curtained doorway. She held a pile of programmes. Big Phil showed his ticket; she tore off the stub. Then he ducked under the curtain and was out of sight.

'Will we go in too?' Flora asked doubtfully.

'Of course.'

The usher nodded them through.

They pushed back the black curtain and stepped beyond.

Andrew gasped.

They were inside the theatre proper.

Far, far down below was the stage. It was lit already, like a frozen lake, in shafts of blue and white. Then came the banks of audience members, rustling and coughing as they took their seats. The expensive seats – where Flora should have been sitting – were on the ground floor. Above those was a balcony, then a second balcony and finally, the gods. And they were looking down at it all. These seats were high enough to give you a nose bleed.

Big Phil was edging his way down a row. He finally settled into a flip-down seat that was right behind a pillar. He had the worst view in the house.

'Well,' Flora whispered, 'he isn't here for the love of theatre.'

Andrew nodded in agreement. Big Phil would see next

to nothing with that pillar in the way. He must be here just to meet Wendy.

Flora checked her ticket. They were on the very end of the very last row. Andrew and Flora slipped into their seats and waited. Wherever Big Phil went, they would be watching.

Chapter Twenty-Three

Piotr took one look at their seats in the auditorium and shook his head. They were right in the centre of the row. 'If we sit there, we'll never be able to sneak out to watch Wendy,' he said.

'But we can't waste the seats,' Minnie said sadly – the view was amazing.

'We have to. Just don't tell Andrew – he'll never forgive us. We need to get in another way.'

They left the auditorium and the foyer, and went around the building to the stage door. There was already a huge crowd of people milling about. They didn't have tickets for the play, but were keen to catch a glimpse of Betty Massino before she went on. They buzzed around the door like wasps around jam.

'How can we get to Wendy?' Minnie asked.

'What we need is a diversion, so that we can get

past security,' Piotr replied.

Minnie grinned. 'I think I can handle that.' She stepped up to the edge of the throng. She pointed towards nothing in particular. 'There she is!' Minnie yelled. 'There's Betty Massino!'

The reaction was instant.

Cries and shrieks and screams went up as the people surged towards Minnie, trying to catch a glimpse of the star. Minnie yelled again, 'Miss Massino, Miss Massino, can I get your autograph?' Then she grabbed Piotr's arm and pulled him up against the theatre wall, beside the stage door.

There were more shrieks from the crowd as toes got trampled and people got shoved.

The stage door shot open and security were out in an instant.

Dave.

He put his hands up in the air, waving for the crowd to be calm.

The crowd was not calm.

Not calm at all.

Dave's timid shouts were lost over the fans'.

Piotr couldn't help thinking that Dad would have handled it better.

But there wasn't time to think about the crowd any more. They slipped behind Dave and his flapping arms, into the theatre.

They rushed right through the lobby into backstage.

The whole place seemed to hum and throb with tension. From the stage area, Piotr could hear the urgent whispers of the stage crew. Nita would be there somewhere, checking final details, making sure the props were in all the right places. Betty would be waiting in her dressing room, eager for the bell to call her to position. Albie would be beside her, making green tea to calm her nerves. And Wendy?

Where would Wendy be?

She might be up in wardrobe, or maybe she'd be by the stage, ready with a needle to rescue any last-minute costume disasters.

'Hey, chaps!' a familiar voice squealed. Sylvie. 'You should get to your seats. The play's going to start soon. I've been practising my lines with Mum, to help her relax.'

Piotr noticed a tall, thin woman with reddy-blonde hair standing in the wings. She was twisting a ring on her finger around and around. Sylvie's mum looked much more nervous than Sylvie.

'Where's Wendy?' Piotr asked. 'Has she met Big Phil? Are we in time?'

'Oh, I'm sorry. I thought I was here to perform onstage, but I suppose I'm only here to be your dogsbody.' Sylvie pressed her lips together and raised an eyebrow.

'Sylvie!' Minnie snapped.

'Fine, fine.' Sylvie dropped her eyebrow back to its normal place. 'Yes, you're in time. Wendy hasn't left the building all day. No one has. It's crazy here. Everyone thinks they've forgotten their lines. Some people are going around barking like dogs to warm up their voices, or chanting like monks to find their Zen space. I don't know why they don't just stop moaning and get on with it. The actor playing the landlord has been sick with nerves, so his costume had to be taken in an inch. Wendy's furious. As usual.'

'Why aren't you nervous?' Piotr asked.

Sylvie gave a scoffing laugh. 'Some of us are professionals.'

'Sylvie, darling.' Her mum had glided towards them, smooth as a dancer. 'You need to be focused now, dear. Time for meditation.'

Sylvie rolled her eyes. 'Stop fussing, Mum.' She grinned at Piotr. 'Wendy's got a temporary wardrobe set up backstage, behind the flats.'

'The flats?' Piotr wondered who lived inside a theatre.

'The set, silly. Wendy's behind the set.'

Piotr nodded gratefully. 'Well, good luck,' he said.

Sylvie gave a small gasp. 'Oh, it's bad luck to wish an actor good luck. You have to say, "Break a leg!"'

'Really?'

'Really.'

'I'll happily wish that you break a leg,' Minnie said. 'Break both of them.'

'Thank you!' Sylvie gave her widest smile and then rushed off into the darkness of the stage, followed by her mother.

Seconds later, the auditorium went dark and the curtain rose.

Chapter Twenty-Four

The twinkling chandeliers that glowed above the audience dimmed. The whisper of voices quieted to a cough or two. There was the odd rustle of chocolate wrappers.

The play was beginning.

Andrew and Flora kept a close watch on the back of Big Phil's head. It bobbed from side to side, trying to get a view of the stage from behind the pillar. The people on either side of him tutted in annoyance.

Onstage, a skinny man was saying something about a Russian orchard.

The audience shuffled on their seats and squished the occasional excited giggle. They were waiting to see Betty. They didn't much care about a Russian orchard.

Then Betty Massino appeared. She swept on like an ocean liner coming into port, her black silk skirts swirling like waves. The jet-black beads around her neck glistened like raven's eyes.

Andrew tried to keep watching Big Phil, but his eyes kept being drawn to the stage.

Betty Massino was wonderful.

She was as elegant as bone china and as sad as bleached bones. Andrew felt tears well up as Betty gave her opening speech.

It was only a quick dig in the ribs from Flora that reminded Andrew they had work to do. He had found himself caring a bit too much about the fruit trees near Moscow.

With the play in full swing, Big Phil reached into his huge leather jacket.

A gun? A tracking device? Andrew craned his neck to see.

A bag of boiled sweets.

Big Phil didn't move from his seat.

Where was the necklace? Were they wrong about Wendy? For the very first time, Andrew wondered whether they might lose Piotr after all.

Chapter Twenty-Five

Backstage was hectic, to make the performance onstage look smooth. Crew in black outfits hissed into radio mics, actors swished props and furniture around in a complicated dance, techies swung scenery flats and lights into position.

Piotr and Minnie did their very best not to get in the way.

Minnie, with her dark clothes and extra height, tried to look as though she were supposed to be there.

Every time someone looked quizzically at Piotr, he just picked up a vase, or a tea urn and looked busy.

There was too much going on for people to pay them much attention.

Sylvie was onstage a lot. She didn't have many lines, but she was often carrying cups, fetching rugs and being a dutiful, grieving daughter. She winked at them once or twice as she bustled past.

'We can't stand here forever,' Minnie hissed. 'We need to find Wendy.'

Piotr nodded. It was time to catch a thief.

They went together to search, past the black curtains that divided the sides of the stage into small sections. In each of these waited an actor or a stagehand with a pile of props, ready for their cues.

The floor was covered in cables and ropes, all taped down with gaffer tape. White tape marked lines and corners all over the black floor. It looked like the stage had fallen off its bike and been covered in plasters.

They found the temporary wardrobe behind the huge scenery.

A metal rail on wheels was pushed against the breeze blocks of the back wall. A loose blanket had been rigged up to make a small changing cubicle. Severe black dresses, tweed suits and lacy jackets hung from the rail.

And beside it all was a wooden chair on which Wendy sat. Her face as stern and unmoving as the grey breeze blocks behind her.

Did she have the necklace? When would she give it to Big Phil?

Piotr knew that if he didn't learn the answers to those

questions, then life from here on in would be entirely in Polish.

They kept back, tucked in the shadows. Watching.

Wendy sat, still as a statue.

Going nowhere.

Chapter Twenty-Six

Andrew and Flora waited for Big Phil to make his move.

He didn't move.

He ate.

Then, when absolutely all the sweets were gone, he finally stood up and headed for the exit.

Chapter Twenty-Seven

Backstage, Wendy's phone rang.

Wendy looked mortified.

From all around came sharp intakes of breath from the cast and crew who could hear the merry tinkling of the ringtone.

Piotr grinned. If keeping your phone on during rehearsals was bad, then keeping it on while the play was live must be a hundred times worse.

Wendy scrambled for her phone and mashed the buttons wildly. The phone was suddenly silent. Then she read the screen to see who was calling. Her hand flew to cover her silent gasp. She stared at the screen in horror.

Wendy stood up.

Then sat back down again.

Then stood up.

She arranged and rearranged the costumes on her rack.

She seemed nervous, frightened even. Then, with a sudden burst of energy, she pushed the costumes along the rack and stalked away from the clothes.

'Now!' Piotr said.

He and Minnie left the stage flat they were hiding behind and ran after Wendy. She moved faster than they could have believed. It was as though her nervousness had turned to anger and she was just looking for someone to get in her way. As long as it wasn't them, Piotr thought.

Wendy stalked past the rest of the crew without speaking a word. Piotr caught a quick glimpse of Nita carrying a crystal lampshade, then she was gone. Wendy flew through the wings, towards the stage door.

And then, took a sharp turn into the ladies'!

Piotr stood staring at the door. At the picture of a woman in a skirt and bonnet. At the word 'ladies' painted in swirly writing.

He couldn't. Could he?

Minnie made up his mind for him. She grabbed his elbow, opened the door and bundled the two of them inside.

There were three cubicles, a row of peach sinks, a thin, white towel on a roll and a small window set high in the wall.

The door to the middle cubicle was shut.

Piotr looked at Minnie in horror.

It was the girls' toilets.

The!

Girls'!

Toilets!

What if someone came in? What if they called the police? Or worse, called his parents?

Then they heard Wendy's voice coming from the middle cubicle – its door was shut. 'How dare you! How dare you call me at work!'

Minnie's eyes widened. She gestured towards the cubicle to the left. With a last, desperate glance at the exit Piotr stepped into the cubicle. Minnie bustled in behind him.

With the door shut, they were as silent as they could be. Shallow breaths. No movement. Willing their heartbeats to slow.

But Wendy was so angry, she wouldn't have noticed a national convention of investigators in the cubicle beside her.

'Philip, this is unacceptable. I know you're my brother and I think the world of you, but you've gone too far.' There was a pause. 'No, no. Betty Massino is a lovely woman and I won't do it. I won't help you. Not again.'

It wasn't just the fact that he was in the girls' toilets that made Piotr flush. Philip. Big Phil.

'Fine. Fine. I'll give you two minutes. Two. That's all,' Wendy snapped. 'Interval.'

They heard a sharp beep as the call ended.

Wendy opened her cubicle door. She stepped out, turned on a tap and splashed some water.

Then they heard the sound of the bathroom door opening and closing.

Wendy had left to make the rendezvous. Piotr and Minnie rushed out of the cubicle to follow her.

Chapter Twenty-Eight

Back on the other side of the curtain, at the top of the staircase to the gods, Andrew and Flora watched Big Phil put away his phone.

He was leaving.

This must be it. The exchange.

The foyer was empty. From the direction of the bar, they could hear the clink of glasses and the shucking of ice – staff preparing interval drinks.

Big Phil trotted down the stairs, across the gilt foyer and out of the front door.

The two crept after him. He didn't look behind him once.

They were nearly outside and into the street when a roar of applause went up behind them – the first half had finished. Soon the audience would be spilling out like rice grains from an upturned jar.

Andrew ran the last few steps. It would be awful to lose Big Phil in a crowd.

And where was Wendy? Was she on her way to meet Phil?

The evening was turning to dusk. The sky was a deep blue, rosed with pink. The trees were black silhouettes; their fairy lights sparkled joyously; they had no idea a hunt was on.

But the hunt *was* on.

Andrew and Flora ducked behind the thick trunk of a plane tree, its bark curled like scorched paper.

Big Phil had stopped next to his little car. He bleeped open the door and squeezed inside. His huge body filled the driver's seat and half of the passenger's seat too. The top of his head scraped the roof. He drummed impatiently on the steering wheel.

He was obviously waiting for someone.

Chapter Twenty-Nine

Wendy headed towards the stage door. She seemed to be powered by fury as she scorched past the crowd outside. Piotr and Minnie had to trot to keep up with her.

Dave gave them a puzzled glance as they ran through the lobby, but he didn't try to stop them.

Piotr was glad. He felt like nothing could stop him now anyway. He was so close to getting the necklace back – to tearing up the flight tickets – that he was almost super-charged. He felt he could stop an enemy with a laser-glare, invincible.

Wendy headed up the side of the theatre, along the road and the avenue of trees. She stopped beside a small car filled with a big man.

She yanked the car door open.

'I told you not to bother me at work, Philip!' Wendy yelled.

Piotr and Minnie crept closer. Then one of the plane trees hissed, 'Psst, over here.' Andrew and Flora.

There really wasn't enough room for all four of them behind the tree, even if they breathed in. But Wendy didn't seem to notice anything other than her brother.

'It isn't fair! I'm trying to get on with my job!' she yelled at the car.

'Has she got the necklace?' Andrew asked.

Piotr felt an icy splinter of fear. Wendy had picked up Big Phil's call, gone to the loos then come straight out here. She hadn't sneaked to a hiding place, or picked up a bag, or anything. She must be wearing the necklace under her clothes, he thought hopefully.

Big Phil eased himself slowly out of the car. 'All right, sis? Show going well, is it? I liked the frocks in the first half. Very fetching.'

'Shut up, Philip. What are you doing here?'

Now Piotr really did feel fear. It was like a sharp fingernail trailing down the back of his neck.

Wendy didn't know why Big Phil was there.

She hadn't known he was coming.

The icy splinter turned into a shard inside Piotr. He couldn't have it wrong. There was too much to lose.

Big Phil rested an elbow on the car roof. The car sank

noticeably. 'This is a golden opportunity. A chance to make our fortunes. You, me and Sparkles.'

A flicker of hope.

Big Phil was talking about a fortune in jewels!

Piotr had to get closer. He had to see the moment when the necklace changed hands. And he had to rugby-tackle Big Phil and pin him down until the police got there.

The lay-by had three more cars tucked neatly against the kerb. Piotr darted from the tree to the nearest car – an SUV with lots of bulk to hide behind.

Wendy and Big Phil were too busy with each other to notice.

'I told you I wouldn't do it, Philip!'

'But think of the pay cheque. This will be big.'

'Think of the risks. They're pretty big too! That's your trouble, Philip – you never think of the consequences.'

Piotr peered around the metal bars attached to the boot of the SUV. He was level with Wendy's waist. She had her hands on her hips, and although she was looking up at her brother, Piotr got the feeling she was also looking down on him.

Big Phil seemed to wilt under his sister's harsh gaze. His shoulders drooped. 'Just take a look, would you? They're exactly like the real thing.'

A forgery?

An exact replica of the necklace?

Piotr risked leaning out a few more inches to see what Big Phil was showing Wendy.

The huge man popped the boot of his car. The whole space was crammed full of cardboard boxes.

Cardboard boxes?

Big Phil lifted the flap on the top box and pulled out a plastic bottle. He held it in front of him, like a prize salmon.

Piotr could read the label clearly.

In pink and yellow swirly writing, it said 'Sparkles'.

'Look, sis, the best slimming product ever! All we need is a big Hollywood star to say they've used it and we'll be coming up roses. Living on Easy Street. Drinking pina coladas on the Costa del Sol.'

Wendy shuddered. 'Philip, that is not a slimming product – it's a bottle of flour with a photocopied label. And, for the very last time, I won't ask Betty Massino to endorse it.'

'Yes, yes, I know it's just flour, but if you just drank water and flour you're bound to lose weight, aren't you?'

Sparkles was a slimming product?

Sparkles was a *fake* slimming product?

Piotr felt the world contract around him, like a throat squeezing closed. He couldn't breathe. He couldn't focus.

The plastic bottles.

The invoice for flour.

The *Slimmers' World* magazine.

All the clues had been in the lock-up. And he'd been too blind to see them.

He slumped against the SUV and felt the cold metal of the bars press against his face.

He'd got it wrong.

He felt a hand on his shoulder and looked up. Minnie. Her eyes reflected back the sadness he felt. She hadn't been sure at the lock-up. He'd talked her into believing Big Phil was the thief.

Andrew reached out too and pulled Piotr to his feet. 'You OK?' Andrew whispered.

Had he really been wrong? Piotr looked at the boot of Big Phil's car, rammed high with boxes.

It wasn't fair.

None of this was fair.

He pushed himself off the SUV and stepped out. 'Hey!' he said.

Wendy and Big Phil both turned. Their look of surprise was identical.

'Do I know you?' Big Phil looked confused.

Piotr planted his feet apart. 'Where's Betty Massino's necklace?' he said.

Big Phil and Wendy looked at each other. Big Phil's mouth hung open so wide a truck could have parked in it. 'We don't know anything about that necklace,' he said. 'I'm a businessman. An honest businessman. And I'll hurt anyone who says otherwise.'

Piotr felt Andrew grab his arm, pull him back, yank him away from the little car. 'Leave it, Piotr. They don't know anything about the necklace.'

Piotr hated to admit it – hated it – but he knew Andrew was right.

Chapter Thirty

There was nothing Piotr could do. It had been stupid to think they could ever get the necklace back. Stupid. The world didn't work that way.

'Come on, Piotr. We need to go,' Minnie said.

Piotr lifted his hand to wave her away, but his legs felt weirdly spongy.

'Lean on me,' Andrew said. Piotr felt an arm loop around his waist. He leaned against his friend. Flora helped too.

'Where are we going?'

'Let's head over to the salon. It's closer than his flat,' Minnie said.

'What about the play?' Andrew asked.

'Well,' Flora said, 'Sylvie told us Betty's character dies at the feast. We're better off not watching it, if you ask me. It sounds depressing.'

They walked in silence. Piotr felt a bit more like

himself as they got nearer the salon. He kept his arm over Andrew's shoulders, though, just to feel close.

Minnie let them in and hit the light switch. The fluorescent tube hummed for a second, then the light flickered on. It illuminated the salon, with all the hair extensions and driers and brushes at one end and the nail bar near the window.

Piotr and Andrew dropped into the window seat. Minnie tucked herself on to a stool by the nail bar. Flora sighed and perched in a chair under a dryer.

'I'm sorry, Piotr. I was so sure we were right,' Flora said. 'It all added up – the weird good-luck card, the "sparkles", the date in the diary.'

Piotr looked out into the dark street. The market was gone, all packed up for the day. Only a few stray bits of rubbish – some squashed fruit, a plastic bag, a bit of frayed rope – showed that it had ever been there. Flora was just trying to make him feel better – he was the one who'd insisted Big Phil was guilty. Who'd led them down the wrong path. Who was going to pay for it when the plane took off tomorrow.

'We've still got two more suspects,' Minnie said hopefully. 'Nita and Albie. We could try and follow them?'

'When?' Piotr snapped. 'It's too late.'

Minnie gasped, as though Piotr had sworn at them all. 'Don't say that. Just don't.'

'It's true, isn't it?' Piotr scowled at the floor.

Flora's dress had a pinafore pouch sewn to the front, like a velvet kangaroo. She reached into it and pulled out her notebook. The place she'd recorded all of their discoveries. 'We should look again. Double-check everything. There might be a crucial detail we've missed. Or something we hadn't thought about before because we were focused on Wendy.'

Piotr kicked his heel against the window seat. 'What's the point?'

'Hey!' Minnie said. 'Don't kick the seat. Mum will go mad. And don't give up so soon. We haven't given up, have we?'

Flora and Andrew both shook their heads.

Piotr felt his eyes grow hot as tears formed. These were his friends. They hadn't judged him when he'd confessed about the card. They'd not doubted him for a second when he'd said Dad was innocent. They were the best friends he could have, and they didn't deserve to have him quit on them.

'OK,' he said, 'there's still time. The play is still on. The flight isn't for hours. Let's have another shot. There might be something we've missed.'

Chapter Thirty-One

Flora opened her notebook.

There were interview notes and the transcription of the conversation she'd recorded with Sylvie. There were printouts of the photos Minnie had taken in wardrobe: hats and wigs, nail varnish and mannequins. There was a plan of the theatre, drawn neatly to scale, with crosses showing where everyone was at the time of the theft.

And there was the list of suspects.

'Was Wendy lying when she said she saw Mr Domek on the stairs, do you think?' Flora said quietly. 'I mean, we assumed she was, because we thought she'd stolen the necklace and was trying to put the blame on someone else. But if she didn't take the necklace …'

'Then she had no reason to lie.' Piotr finished her sentence for her. 'So, she must have seen my dad on the stairs. But he says he was in the wings, so she can't have. It doesn't make sense,'

Andrew sat up straight suddenly, as though he'd been bitten on the behind. He gave a small yelp. Then he started fishing around in his pockets.

'Are you OK?' Minnie asked.

Andrew ignored her. He was pulling things out of his pockets: sweet wrappers, tissues, his play ticket, and then, a tightly folded page from a newspaper. He worked quickly to unfold it, then smoothed it flat on the nail bar.

Piotr recognised the page. It showed Betty Massino arriving at the theatre, stepping out of a black car outside the stage door. It was torn from the newspaper Andrew had brought to the salon on the day Betty arrived.

'I know why Wendy would say she saw Piotr's dad when she didn't,' Andrew said, thrusting the paper at Minnie. 'Look!'

'Why are you carrying a clipping from the newspaper in your pocket?' Piotr asked.

Andrew reddened a little. 'I was going to ask Betty Massino to sign it – you know, if the time was right. It doesn't matter. Look!' He pointed at a person in the background of the photo: a man in a dark jumper, with slicked back dark hair and grey pinstripe trousers, carrying two suitcases and wearing a scowl on his face.

Albie.

'If you'd gone upstairs to fetch your glasses so you weren't wearing them yet, and you saw the back of Albie's head, with his dark hair and dark grey jumper heading away from you, what might you think?'

'That you'd seen my dad!' Piotr exclaimed.

'Exactly!' Andrew said. 'And if you were Albie Sandbaum, who wanted to stay in LA, who wasn't getting the breaks you thought you deserved, if you were tired and angry with your boss and too poor to quit, what might you do?'

'Steal a diamond necklace,' Flora whispered.

'We need to find Albie Sandbaum,' Piotr said.

Chapter Thirty-Two

Flora checked her watch. 'The interval will be over in three minutes. We have to get back to the theatre.'

They needed no second invitation. Everyone leaped up. Andrew grabbed his newspaper cutting. They hurtled out of the salon like Formula One drivers vying for pole position. There was a tight logjam at the door, then they were all running, as fast as they could, down the street to the theatre.

A few stragglers in suits hung around the main doors, but the crowd of theatre-goers were all but gone. 'The second half is about to begin,' Flora gasped.

'Where will Albie be? In the auditorium?'

Flora shook her head. 'He's there to help Betty. He'll be backstage, in her dressing room making tea or standing ready with a shawl or something.'

Piotr looked up at the imposing wall of the theatre,

with its frost-icing mouldings and columns. 'We've just come from backstage. We can't get back in there again.'

Were they stuck on the outside? While the thief carried shawls, tea and on regardless?

'There is something we could do,' Flora said. She pulled out her phone and dialled. 'Mum? Are you with Sylvie? ... Yes, yes, I'm fine ... I know she's in beginner's position. Can I speak to her? Please? No, it's important ... Sylvie? Listen ...'

Chapter Thirty-Three

Flora spoke. Sylvie listened. Then Flora said, 'You can? You're a star.' Flora hung up. She gave a wide grin. 'Come on!'

Flora ran past the main entrance, down the alley, through the crowd at the stage door, following the wall beyond. Small windows were set high up in the wall, like arrow slits in a castle keep.

One of the windows opened.

Sylvie's face peered out.

The window was two metres off the ground. Not even Minnie could stretch far enough to reach the sill.

'Give me a boost,' Minnie told Andrew.

He cupped his palms. Minnie stepped up and sprang at the sill. Sylvie ducked out of the way just in time, while Minnie scrambled through. It was part-slither, part-fall as she landed in a tangled heap on the floor of the ladies' toilets.

'Are you OK?' Piotr called from outside.

Minnie sat up on the chequered tiles, rubbed a bruised thigh, then went to the window. 'I'm fine. Come on up!'

Andrew gave a boost to Flora and Piotr, while Minnie pulled them through from above. Then Minnie hung as far out of the window as she could, gripped Andrew's wrists and hoisted him up to join the others.

Piotr glanced around the room. He'd never been in the ladies' toilets before today and here he was, for the second time in one night.

Sylvie, in a long gown and elaborate hairdo, tutted at them all. 'You have perfectly good seats in the second row. Expensive seats. Why you have to climb in through a bathroom window, I have no idea.'

Flora grinned. 'It's our SAS training.'

'Ha ha. Are you loving the play? Isn't Betty wonderful? Did you hear my lines? I was a bit croaky at first, but then I think I sounded great. Well … ?' She looked from one face to the next, waiting for praise.

'Shouldn't you be onstage right about now?' Minnie asked.

Sylvie yelped. 'I'm supposed to serve the wine at the feast!'

She hoisted up her skirt and ran out of the toilets as though her shoes were on fire.

'Right,' Piotr said, 'we're in. Now we need to find Albie and get the necklace back.'

Chapter Thirty-Four

They crept out of the toilets. Piotr took the lead, watching out for Dave, or any of the crew, or, in fact, anyone who'd have them thrown out. He avoided the stage completely. He headed towards the staircase that led up to the company dressing rooms, and, above those, the principal dressing rooms.

The corridors were strangely silent.

All the cast were onstage for the second half.

Piotr's steps slowed as he reached Betty's room. The door was shut. Should they go in? Should they really accuse her assistant of stealing? They had no proof. No evidence. Just a coincidence of clothing. He'd been wrong before. Was he wrong this time too?

Minnie stumbled into his back as he came to a stop.

'What is it?' she asked in a whisper. 'What's wrong?'

Piotr bit his lip gently. 'We need to be certain this

time. We'll just hear what he has to say and decide what to do then.'

Then he found himself knocking on the dressing-room door.

'Yes?' The door opened to reveal Albie, slouching against the frame, all angles and joints. 'Oh, it's the Small-Scale Scoobies. Did Betty forget something?' he drawled.

Even his American accent was intimidating.

'We wondered ...' Piotr began. Then he realised he didn't know what to say. 'We wondered ...'

'What?' Albie snapped.

Piotr took a breath. He could do this. 'Andrew, show him the newspaper.'

Andrew whipped the picture out of his pocket and handed it across.

Albie held the rumpled paper in his long fingers for a moment. He peered at it as though he could see germs crawling across the surface. 'Betty arriving. What about it?'

'It's your jumper,' Andrew said. 'That dark grey colour looks an awful lot like a security guard's jumper. Don't you think?'

'What security guard?' Albie frowned.

Piotr found that he was shaking. Did Albie really not

know? 'My dad!' It was practically a shout. Piotr squished the emotion; he had to stay in control. 'My dad, the security guard,' he said. 'Wendy swore that she saw him hiding in the company dressing rooms corridor when she came up the main stairs. But in that grey jumper –'

'It's charcoal,' Albie interrupted, 'the colour is called charcoal. And it's a sweater.'

'In that charcoal sweater, someone with bad eyesight, like Wendy, could easily have confused you for my dad.'

'Me?' Albie's hands flew to his chest. The newspaper crumpled alarmingly. 'How could you confuse me with a security guard? That sweater is cashmere!'

Piotr squared his shoulders and looked Albie right in the eye. 'Were you up here when the necklace was stolen?'

Albie's mouth curled into a sneer. 'How dare you? How dare you come up here and accuse me of stealing from Betty? I owe everything to her. When she met me, I was just some kid hanging around Los Angeles trying to get a break. She took me in, gave me hope –'

'That's not what you said the other day,' Andrew interrupted. 'You said you couldn't stand your job.'

Albie sneered. 'You can't prove anything. Who cares what I said to a snotty little kid? You've no evidence, because I didn't do it.'

'So, you wouldn't mind if we gave this picture to the police? You wouldn't mind taking part in an identity parade at the police station for Wendy?' Piotr asked.

Albie's eyes darted left, then right.

And then he moved.

Albie rushed out of the dressing room, knocking Piotr aside and sprinting hard down to the far end of the corridor. He flew through a door marked with a running man and galloped down the back stairs.

'The fire exit! Andrew, Flora, back the way we came. Cut him off. Minnie, after him!' Piotr yelled.

He set off after Albie with Minnie right behind him.

Albie was trying to make a run for it.

They were crashing down the fire escape now.

The sound of heavy footsteps echoed up. Piotr saw flashes of movement, a dark sleeve grabbing a handrail, a black shoe leaping down steps. Albie had a good lead. But Piotr and Minnie were fit, and keen to catch him.

Piotr forced his legs to move up a gear. Each step was a springboard to the next. Faster and faster.

Albie was in view now.

Piotr stretched out. His arm so close to Albie's back …

Grabbing thin air.

Albie dodged right.

The fire exit came into view. Albie was nearly out!

Then from the other direction, Andrew and Flora flew in front of the door.

Albie skidded to a halt, glanced around, then took off again.

Towards the stage.

Piotr saw him dart towards the black flats that surrounded the backstage area. His charcoal top blended like a black cat at midnight. Hurried cries and sharp whispers came from the crew as they suddenly noticed him running in the darkness.

Piotr and the others were in hot pursuit.

Albie neared the glare of the stage lights. He glanced back. His terrified face shone with sweat. He looked at the stage, where a feast was being served, and at the audience beyond. Back at the children. Back at the stage. He was stuck. He couldn't go forward, he couldn't go back.

They had him cornered.

Chapter Thirty-Five

Albie was trapped. Caught between Piotr and the stage.

And then he took one huge leap.

From the wings ... right into the play.

Albie had entered the performance!

The actor speaking paused for a split second as he caught sight of the assistant, then, ever the professional, carried on with his lines.

The audience rustled, gave soft murmurs, wondering whether Albie was part of the action.

Then Albie rushed forwards, heading towards the edge of the stage and the freedom of the auditorium.

'Stop him!' Piotr shouted.

Sylvie, who was standing upstage, holding a wine bottle, responded immediately.

She poked her dainty, booted foot out, right in Albie's path.

He tripped, stumbled and smacked head first on to the cold, hard boards.

This was his chance! Piotr dashed out of the wings, dropped to his knees and landed on top of Albie.

Sylvie stepped back into position.

The audience gasped. Sylvie pretended not to notice, though her cheeks flushed a little pink.

Piotr stayed on top of Albie, who writhed and wriggled beneath him.

A voice spoke from the edge of the stage. 'Looks like you need a bit of help?'

Piotr looked up into the face of Jimmy Wright.

'He stole it!' Piotr said, trying hard not to let Albie squirm his way free.

'The necklace?' Jimmy asked.

Piotr nodded fiercely.

Jimmy pressed his finger to the earpiece he was wearing and spoke urgently. 'Back-up requested immediately to stage.'

The audience was murmuring loudly now and there were even camera flashes.

The actors held their positions onstage, faces as blank as statues.

Jimmy nodded to Piotr to stand. Then he grabbed

Albie's arms, lifted him to his feet and held him tight.

'It was the charcoal cashmere,' Piotr said. 'Ask him about that. His sweater. Hold an identity parade. You'll need Wendy.'

'Slow down,' Jimmy said.

From the corner of his eye, Piotr saw Andrew, Minnie and Flora edge on to the stage.

On the other side, he saw Wendy and Nita hovering, probably closer to the spotlight than they'd ever been before.

And, in front of him, the rows and banks and layers of people. The audience. All looking at him. Like judges in evening gowns and suits, watching every move. He felt panic rise up inside him. What if he was wrong again?

'Look at me,' Jimmy said.

Piotr forced himself to turn around, to look away from the hundreds of pairs of eyes and into just one pair of hazel-green, kindly eyes – Jimmy's.

Jimmy gave a small smile. 'You think Albie took it? Do you know how? Do you know where it is?'

No.

He didn't know.

He hadn't the slightest clue.

Albie must have seen the look of horror on Piotr's face, because he gave a short, barking laugh. 'They don't know where it is any more than I do. I'm innocent. I'll get the US Embassy involved. You'll all be thrown in jail for assault.' Albie glared at Sylvie and rubbed his forehead. 'Especially you,' he added.

At the side of the stage, Minnie, Andrew and Flora looked at one another. They'd stopped the play. They'd ruined opening night. And they had no evidence. Or the necklace.

Albie was right. They were in worse trouble than any of them had ever dreamed possible. This was all the detentions and letters home and groundings in the world come at once.

'My mum is going to kill me,' Minnie whispered. 'Unless we work out where Albie hid the necklace.'

Piotr glanced at Albie standing beside Jimmy. He was sweaty from running, his hair was all mussed up and a bruise was developing on his forehead. It was strange seeing him so flustered, so untidy. He was normally so prim and perfect.

Except he wasn't. Not always.

He remembered the notes Flora had taken.

Andrew had noticed Albie's black fingernails.

Minnie had found black varnish in wardrobe.

Flora had learned that Nita hadn't touched the accessories boxes.

Piotr looked out at the audience – and smiled. He wasn't frightened any more.

He stepped into the very centre of the stage. The landlord stepped aside. A spotlight swung around from somewhere up above and halted on Piotr, pooling him in white light.

To his right, Andrew, Minnie and Flora covered their eyes – they couldn't watch.

To his left, Betty Massino was still sitting patiently, waiting for the rumpus to be over and her scene to restart.

'Ladies and gentlemen,' Piotr said.

'Speak up,' someone shouted from the gods.

'Ladies and gentlemen!' Piotr yelled. 'Earlier this week, a diamond necklace was stolen from one of our most talented performers. Wendy – who works in wardrobe – reported seeing Mr Domek fleeing the scene of the crime. But Wendy has terrible eyesight. What she saw was the fleeing back of none other than Albie – Betty's not-so-devoted assistant.'

The audience muttered. Piotr raised his hands; he hadn't finished.

'Ladies and gentlemen, Albie wasn't fleeing the scene with the necklace in his pocket. No! He had hidden it *inside the theatre*.'

Jimmy shook his head. 'We searched every inch.'

'You searched every inch for a hidden *diamond* necklace. But Albie had taken some black nail varnish from Betty's dressing room and painted the diamonds. He was clumsy and got it under his fingernails – he left the top off!'

Betty couldn't hold her pose at the table any longer. She stood up, clattering the plates on the table as she did. She looked at Albie. 'You no-good, sneaky, underhand, lying snake!' she shouted. 'Where are my diamonds?'

Piotr glanced at Minnie. She nodded and gave him a huge grin. She knew the answer too.

Minnie stepped on to the stage. 'Miss Massino, if you'd allow me?' She moved to the table and picked up a sharp knife with an ornate handle – the dagger meant for the heart of the landlord. She moved towards the actress. She held up the dagger. She lifted the jet necklace that Betty was wearing and scraped the knife along one of the black beads.

The black coating came off on the blade, like crayon wax.

Underneath, the sparkle of diamonds shone brightly under the stage lights.

The audience burst into a deafening round of applause.

Chapter Thirty-Six

The play didn't continue after that. Too many people were on their feet applauding the action – Andrew, Betty, Minnie, Piotr, even Nita and Wendy were pushed onstage to curtsy awkwardly.

Albie was led away by the back-up police officers. The necklace was taken into evidence. They were hoping the nail varnish had preserved any fingerprints below – Albie's fingerprints.

Eventually, the audience filed out into the street. The cast left the stage and it was just Jimmy, Betty and the gang left.

'So, the diamonds never left the theatre?' Jimmy said in wonder. 'But the sniffer dog?'

'The nail varnish must have masked Betty's scent,' Piotr said.

Betty Massino hadn't stopped smiling since Minnie

had come at her with the dagger. 'You found them,' she said. 'You guys are really amazing. I can't believe Albie would hide them from me.'

Andrew shook his head. 'He wasn't just hiding them. I saw him reading a costume magazine. He had to steal the diamonds before you took them to the bank but I bet he was having a replica set of black beads made. As soon as it was done, he was planning to switch the diamonds for the replica. Stealing them twice!'

Betty looked shocked. 'I thought he was my friend,' she said softly.

'I'm sorry,' Minnie put her hand on Betty's arm.

It was funny to think that even a world-famous actor needed friends.

'And I'm sorry,' Wendy told Nita. 'I blamed you for touching the necklaces in wardrobe – when it was Albie all along.'

'That's all right,' Nita said. 'I never liked him, did you?' She slipped her arm through Wendy's. The two headed offstage together.

'What will happen to him now?' Betty asked.

'I'll need to take statements from the children,' Jimmy said. 'I think I'll have a look at Flora's brilliant notebook. And we'll need to take prints from the bottle of nail polish too. If we can link it to Albie we'll be close to getting a conviction.'

'Does that mean my dad's in the clear?'

Jimmy's face flushed. 'I think we owe your dad an apology. Shall I walk you home? Have a word with him in person?'

Piotr nodded.

'I just need to talk to the duty officer first. Wait here.'

Betty stood up. 'I'd better get out of costume. Wendy will string me like beans if I ruin this dress. Will you come back tomorrow? Watch the play properly, as my guests?'

Piotr looked at the ground. 'I don't know,' he said. 'I don't know where I'll be tomorrow.'

'Well,' Betty said, 'there's a ticket with your name on it, if you can.'

Jimmy and Betty left the group alone. Flora and Sylvie linked arms and rested their heads together. They were tired. Minnie sat on the stage and tucked her knees under her chin. Andrew and Piotr dropped down beside her. The huge auditorium with its rows and rows of red velvet seats spread around the stage in a grin.

'We did it,' Andrew said softly. 'We really did it. Do you think Betty could get us a part in her next film, to say thank you?'

Minnie tutted at him. 'Will we see you in the morning, Piotr?' she asked.

'I guess that depends on how good the police are at apologising,' Piotr said, thinking of the plane tickets to Poland stuck to the fridge.

Chapter Thirty-Seven

Piotr waited outside in the dark hallway. The living-room door had been closed for about half an hour, with Mum, Dad and Jimmy shut up behind it. He couldn't make out the words, but Dad's clipped voice was clear, contrasting with Jimmy's softer one. Mum only spoke occasionally, asking questions of both men.

Would it be enough?

They'd found the necklace, but Dad hadn't been happy here anyway. He'd felt like an outsider, a stranger. He'd felt the way that Piotr would feel in Poland. Perhaps Dad would decide that the time was right to leave, even with an apology.

Piotr sat down on the rough carpet and rested his head on his knees.

The waiting was awful.

He couldn't stand it any more. He got up and pushed

open the living-room door. Inside, Dad and Jimmy were on the sofa. Mum was sitting in the armchair.

'Pietrucha,' Dad said.

Was that a good sign?

Piotr tried to read the adults' faces. Trying to see his future in the slant of an eyebrow, the curl of a smile.

He couldn't tell.

So he'd just have to ask. 'Are we going to Poland?'

'Yes,' Mum said. 'What are you doing still up? It's going to be a long day tomorrow.'

It couldn't be true. He glared at Jimmy. 'You were supposed to apologise.'

Jimmy held up his hands. 'I have. I promise I have!'

Piotr looked at Dad. 'Then why are we still leaving?'

'We can't waste the plane tickets,' Dad said. 'But don't worry. I won't be looking for work; we won't ask about schools. It will just be for a holiday. We'll go and see your cousins and be back home in ten days. How does that sound?'

Piotr threw himself at Dad and wrapped his arms around him.

'He felt Dad's warm, heavy hand on his back. 'I'm so proud of you, Pietrucha. You fought for what you wanted. You were right: I was just running away.'

'No, you weren't –'

'Shh, it's OK. I was. But you stopped me.'

Piotr buried his face in the spice scent of Dad. 'Thank you,' Piotr whispered.

'I'll be off then,' Jimmy said, with a faint trace of embarrassment. 'You'll think about what I said, Mr Domek? About the force?'

Dad rested a hand on Piotr's head for a second, then stood up. He and Jimmy moved towards the hall. 'I'll think about it, yes.'

Jimmy gave Piotr a quick wink, then was gone.

'What did he mean, *the force*?' Piotr asked.

Mum gave a short laugh. 'It seems they need Polish speakers as special constables. They're recruiting. Jimmy wondered if your dad might be interested.'

'Dad's going to be a police officer?'

'Maybe,' she said. 'I don't know. It might suit him. Now, you'd better get some rest. You're going on holiday in the morning.'

Before they left for the airport, Piotr had enough time to run to the salon. Minnie and Andrew were both there. Andrew was poring over a newspaper as Piotr burst into the shop.

'Piotr! You're still here!' Minnie leaped up to hug him.

Andrew dropped the paper and practically rugby-tackled Piotr.

'Oof! Yes, I'm here for good. Though we are going on holiday today.'

'We did it! We really did it!' Minnie shimmied across the salon floor.

'And we're in the paper!' Andrew flapped the front page in front of Piotr's face. There was a photograph of them onstage, with Betty Massino sitting in the background. 'They've called it a "wonderful, immersive performance, with mixed media elements", and given it five stars. Look!'

Piotr looked at his friends.

He was staying.

They'd done it.

'Will you call Flora and Sylvie and say thank you from me?' he asked.

Minnie nodded.

'I'd better go. Mum said I only had five minutes to say goodbye.'

'It's OK,' Minnie said. 'Now we know you're coming back.'

Piotr gave them both another rough hug. He yelled goodbye to Minnie's mum. He launched himself through the salon door and, as he ran past the market stalls, the shouts of the shoppers, the colours and smells and sounds of Marsh Road – his home – he realised that he was smiling. '*Na razie!*' he shouted. 'See you soon!'

Read on for some

top-secret character stats

on the Marsh Road

investigators!

PIOTR DOMEK

Somehow, to his surprise, Piotr leads the gang of investigators. He isn't sure quite how that happened – the job just landed on him. Luckily, he wasn't hurt. Now, with his dad's reputation at stake, he has to put down his comic books and pick up the reins. Who knows where he might end up?

Brain power: **8**

Friendship factor: **9**

Honesty: **10**

Bravery: **9**

Sleuthing: **8**

Self-confidence: **5**

MINNIE ADESINA

Minnie is as tall and as prickly as the branches of a holly tree, but her heart is firmly in the right place. Once she's your friend, she's your friend forever. On rainy days, when there's no mystery to be solved, Minnie can be found treating Mum's nail polishes like magic potions. It almost counts as a hobby.

Brain power: 7
Friendship factor: 10
Honesty: 6
Bravery: 9
Sleuthing: 7
Self-confidence: 8

ANDREW JONES

The whole world is a stage, as far as Andrew is concerned, and he is the leading man. And every other role too, if he can get his hands on the script. He loves to be the centre of attention and is always ready to take a risk. In his less dramatic moments, he helps take care of his mum.

Brain power: 7
Friendship factor: 8
Honesty: 5
Bravery: 10
Sleuthing: 8
Self-confidence: 9

FLORA HAMPSHIRE

Good things come in small packages, and there are few people as good as the youngest twin (by five minutes) Flora. She's always ready with a kind word, or a helping hand, or a disgusting fact if that's what the situation calls for. Her book of forensic science is never far from reach. And her note-taking is the very best in the business.

Brain power: 10

Friendship factor: 9

Honesty: 9

Bravery: 6

Sleuthing: 9

Self-confidence: 4

SYLVIE HAMPSHIRE

The older of the two twins (by five minutes), Diva is Sylvie Hampshire's middle name. As a promising young actress, she demands the limelight. She'd rather be making waves than making friends. As long as her blood sugar is fine, there's nothing that can stop her getting to the top. It's been that way ever since Mum and Dad split up.

Brain power: **7**
Friendship factor: **3**
Honesty: **4**
Bravery: **9**
Sleuthing: **6**
Self-confidence: **10**

Look out for the next instalment of

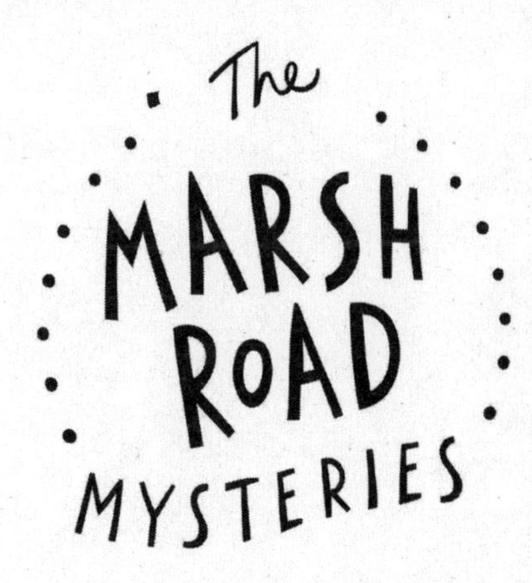

Crowns and Codebreakers

Coming summer 2015